"Jennifer, why are you still fighting me?" Stephen called out angrily to her.

"You're still running scared, and I don't for the life of me know what you're so frightened of. I thought, especially after this morning . . ."

Was he trying to use the beautiful experience they had shared as a ploy in some manipulative game he was playing? "I don't know what you want," she said quietly. "Except sex, of course. Maybe that's *all* you want."

"Isn't this what *you* want?" he demanded, pulling her against him, his mouth bearing down on hers, his tongue probing, insistent. She arched back against him, responding in spite of herself to his passionate demands. For a wild instant she remembered the rapturous abandon of their night together.

"Think about it, Jennifer," he said, his voice hard and cold. "Remember that you're never going to get what you want until you know what it is."

Dear Reader:

As the months go by, we continue to receive word from you that SECOND CHANCE AT LOVE romances are providing you with the kind of romantic entertainment you're looking for. In your letters you've voiced enthusiastic support for SECOND CHANCE AT LOVE, you've shared your thoughts on how personally meaningful the books are, and you've suggested ideas and changes for future books. Although we can't always reply to your letters as quickly as we'd like, please be assured that we appreciate your comments. Your thoughts are all-important to us!

We're glad many of you have come to associate SECOND CHANCE AT LOVE books with our butterfly trademark. We think the butterfly is a perfect symbol of the reaffirmation of life and thrilling new love that SECOND CHANCE AT LOVE heroines and heroes find together in each story. We hope you keep asking for the "butterfly books," and that, when you buy one—whether by a favorite author or a talented new writer—you're sure of a good read. You can trust all SECOND CHANCE AT LOVE books to live up to the high standards of romantic fiction you've come to expect.

So happy reading, and keep your letters coming!

With warm wishes,

Ellen Edwards

Ellen Edwards
SECOND CHANCE AT LOVE
The Berkley/Jove Publishing Group
200 Madison Avenue
New York, NY 10016

STARLIT SEDUCTION
ANNE REED

SECOND CHANCE AT LOVE
BOOK

STARLIT SEDUCTION

STARLIT SEDUCTION

chapter 1

AT LAST SOME SUN! Jennifer Denning smiled like a contented kitten as she stretched out on a comfortable chaise, luxuriating in the feel of the warming rays on her back. Opening one lazy eye, she again surveyed the broad slate terrace of the magnificent sixteenth-century villa that was to be her home—at least for the summer. She knew that if she sat up and peered beyond the terrace wall she'd see the city of Florence in all its glory. But at the moment sleep was more enticing than the stunning view, a sleep that would ease not only her jet lag, but also her other, deeper aches. She shifted lazily, rested her head on a crooked arm, and was ready to drift off.

"*Scusi, signorina.*" Her peace was shattered by the deep, brisk voice. The words were perfectly polite, the form of address appropriately formal, but the tone bordered on arrogant. Though she was embarrassed at being caught sunbathing in a skimpy bikini, she'd be damned if she'd let the owner of that voice know how much he'd startled her. Mustering every ounce of dignity she possessed, she rolled over gracefully and propped herself up on one elbow, shading her eyes with the other hand.

"*Si?* May I help you with something?" she asked coldly in perfect Italian. Yet, as the words left her mouth, she was forced to stifle a gasp. Standing with his back to the sun, the man appeared as a muscular, well-sculpted silhouette. The impact of his presence was such that he seemed like a latter-day Colossus of Rhodes. His long, muscular legs—encased in tight, faded blue jeans—were planted firmly on the ground, slightly apart, so she had the impression he was almost straddling her. His hands, resting almost insolently on his hips, completed his arrogant pose. A tremor of fear ran through her as she realized the distinct disadvantage she had in her horizontal position.

Seemingly unaware of her discomfort—infuriatingly unaware—the man ran his eyes admiringly over her slender body clad only in the brilliantly striped bikini, which left little to the imagination. The frankness of his appraisal forced her into action, and she rose quickly and stepped over to a bench, where she had tossed a matching bright red and yellow cover-up. She slipped it over her head defiantly, then turned back to face the stranger.

For a second time she was struck by the man's appearance. He had the hard body of a man who must do a fair amount of physical labor, and the most devasting ice-blue eyes she had ever seen.

"Don't interrupt your sunbath on my account, please," he said in soft Italian, a trace of the local accent in his voice—and a glimmer of provocative amusement in his eyes. Unlike his first words, these were more mocking than bold. He continued, "I was enjoying it as much as you, signorina...?"

"Denning," she snapped, refusing to be softened by his insinuating banter. What nerve! She had run into annoying, persistent Italian men when she had been in Italy before, but now that she had moved to Florence, one of the world's most civilized cities, she had somehow expected to be shown a little more respect. This man probably thought she was a naïve American tourist. She'd set him straight, and right away!

"Sono Signora Denning," she repeated pointedly, emphasizing the word *"Signora"*—"Mrs." She was aware that his penetrating glance fell instantly to her bare ring finger, but she continued to speak quickly in fluent Italian, adding touches from the local dialect to let him know that she wasn't new to his country— and that his presence didn't fluster her.

"I'm a teacher in the summer program here at the villa," she explained. She glanced again at his suntanned, worker's body. "And you? May I ask what you're doing here? This *is* private property." Made suddenly wary by the thought that he probably didn't belong here, she moved casually across the terrace closer to the french doors.

His blue eyes locked onto her green ones. "I have the right to be here," he said firmly. His tone forbade her from asking him further questions. For a moment, silence reigned on the sunlit terrace, along with a tension so strong that Jennifer felt she could hardly breathe.

Then the man spoke again, easing the spell he'd cast. "I am working to build the cottages for the students down by the olive grove. The actual work hasn't started, but I am here to help make preparations, and to reassure the people on the property that the noise they'll soon be hearing comes from the construction." He moved close to her, and she felt the heat his body generated. "You don't look at all reassured, *Signora* Denning." His tone was amused rather than concerned, and she noticed the way he'd said *"Signora"* — as if he knew it no longer stood for a married state, but was something she used to hide behind.

"Your appearance startled me, that's all," Jennifer replied. She couldn't tear her gaze away from the compelling stranger, whose eyes were the most striking feature in a chiseled face dominated by a Roman nose, which gave him a hawklike quality. His shiny black hair was just long enough to soften the sharpness of his looks. His deeply tanned skin made his eyes seem lighter than they were. The looks were typically European, she decided. And he probably had a young wife and at least several little *bambini* at home, she added to herself.

He made a move toward the wall, and she again looked directly at him — whether to show him she wasn't afraid, or just to get a better look, she couldn't decide. His eyes held hers for a long moment without wavering, and then he grinned, nodded as if in mock-surrender, sprang up onto the wall surrounding the terrace, and vanished over the hill in the direction of the olive groves.

Jennifer stood where he'd left her for an instant, then shook her shiny, shoulder-length blond hair impatiently, her gray-green eyes clouding over, and turned back toward the villa. She felt exhausted, as if she and the stranger had been engaged in some kind of battle. But at the same time she felt strangely light headed, her cares banished momentarily, replaced by an odd excitement.

She caught herself up sharply. No sense in daydreaming about a man she'd probably never see again, especially one who so obviously came from a world entirely different from her own. He seemed to be the typical Italian macho, barging in on her like that. Perhaps she should even report him to someone—but then, she realized with a start, she'd been too stunned to even get his name.

For an instant she wondered what it was—Giancarlo? Marcello? Why did only movie stars' names come to mind? "Wait a minute," she warned herself out loud. What she really needed was a calm, peaceful summer, she reminded herself, a chance to get into teaching and decide whether that was what she wanted to do with her life. What she *didn't* need was a mysterious, arrogant Italian with the power to leave her breathless. She was *not* going to repeat old mistakes.

She removed the cover-up and stretched out again on the chaise, but couldn't shake the feeling that the stranger was still there, watching her, laughing. Finally she got up and walked around the corner of the terrace, down the stone steps and through the magnificent formal garden toward the pool. A less intrepid soul might think it a little too early in the day for a swim, but Jennifer knew she wouldn't mind the cold water. In fact, at the moment she would welcome it.

Walking toward the deep end, she stopped before reaching the diving board to savor the incredible view. The rusts and ochres of the buildings of Florence leaped up at her, as if off the brush of a great artist. It seemed as if she could reach out and touch the city, and she knew she would never tire of looking at it.

Forgetting her swim for the time being, she walked across the cool grass to an ancient retaining wall. Leaning against it, she drank in the scene, enjoying the warmth of the sun-baked stones against her thighs and the weathered texture of the bricks. The city gleamed in the sun, a crazy quilt of red-tiled roofs and sandstone buildings sprawled along both shores of the dark blue River Arno. Far away, yet crystal clear, was the Ponte Vecchio, one of several bridges that spanned the river, this one occupied by artisans' houses and shops, looking exactly as it must have in the Middle Ages. Nearer, dominating the scene, was the massive bulk of the Duomo, the cathedral.

"I think I could look at it forever," said a deep, newly familiar voice behind her. "It's a perfect city, and beautifully preserved. Especially now that cars are banned from the center. Parts are just as Dante must have seen them; much of it, just as the Medici family built it."

Jennifer had again been startled by the sound of his voice, but she quickly forgot that feeling as she considered his words. He must be about five years older than she was, somewhere in his early thirties. He was too old to be a student working for the summer. Then she scolded herself. Just because he was a laborer didn't mean he couldn't be moved by the amazing beauty of the city which, judging from his accent, he'd most likely lived in for most of his life.

She wondered if he'd ever had much chance to travel. "Have you ever seen Rome?" she asked, and was taken by surprise when he burst into laughter.

"Of course I've seen it," he said. A certain expression crossed his face—was it anger, she asked herself, at her seeming condescension?

He raised his head and thrust back his shoulders, assuming a proud stance. "I mean, of course I've had chance to see it," he said, "though now, with the *bambini . . .*" He shrugged. She noticed that his accent had become heavier, his speech less grammatical, and she was embarrassed for having asked him about Rome in the first place.

To make up for the question, she stepped over to the satchel she'd carried out with her, and pulled out a roll of expensive hard candies that she'd picked up in the Rome airport. She turned, only to be startled again to find him standing right behind her, his catlike grace having brought him there noiselessly.

"Here," she said, extending the candies and refusing to look into his eyes, "for the *bambini.*"

He took them from her, and she noticed that he seemed genuinely moved. *"Grazie,"* he said.

Still keeping her gaze away from his, she walked back to the wall and the vista beyond, eager to change the subject. Again he was immediately beside her. "You keep surprising me, signor," she told him. "Do you make a habit of sneaking up on people?"

"Only if they're easily distracted," he replied. He moved closer, and a tingle of excitement coursed through her. "I suspect you are a dreamer, signora, a true romantic." He fingered a lock of her golden hair, and she drew in her breath. "You seem lost in your own thoughts much of the time."

This was too much. She shook her head, and though his hand fell from her hair, the satisfied smile on his face told her he knew of her discomfort. She took a step away.

"Well, I am by myself at the moment—or at least I *was!*" She tried to glare at him. "What would you have me do?" she requested tartly. "Talk to the statues? Of course I become absorbed in my own thoughts."

He ignored her sharp tone. "When I look out over the city, signora, I daydream that there might still be some Medici around—to commission equally grand buildings that *I* can work on." He laughed. "So you see? We all have our fantasies." His skin crinkled attractively at the corners of his mocking blue eyes.

Despite his charms, Jennifer didn't want to discuss dreams and fantasies with a virtual stranger. Again she changed the subject. "Have you finished your work for the day?"

"Yes. We took some final measurements. The heavy machinery will be coming in on Monday. But don't worry—we're doing as little damage to the countryside as possible. We won't touch a single olive tree." His eyes twinkled. "I trust you approve, signora?"

"Yes . . . of course," she stammered. She had just been wondering whether the construction would harm any of the beautiful surroundings of the villa. Did this man read minds in his spare time? He burst into laughter at her confusion, and Jennifer found herself blushing.

He seemed only to relax more when he saw her lack of ease. "Actually," he explained, "I came over here to tell you we were leaving. But I must admit I was also hoping for a swim. In my life you know—" and again he made a gesture of resignation "—there are not many ways to find pleasure. And when working on a job like this, well, I think you Americans call it a 'fringe benefit.'" His penetrating look made Jennifer think that perhaps he considered her another. The idea was frightening.

She hadn't even thought about being desired by a man for what seemed like a very long time, but his gaze was so compelling that she found herself wondering what his lips would feel like. Would they be hard, like his sculpted profile and his lean, muscular body? Or light, like his bantering manner? She forced herself to look away. His closeness was unsettling. The butterflies in her stomach were fluttering madly. She exhaled softly, regathering her control.

Suddenly, with no warning, he bent over and kissed her softly. His mouth was like velvet—exquisite, silken, and gentle. Jennifer felt as though her lips were on fire; she wanted the kiss to last forever. Then the pressure of his mouth increased, making her aware of the thrilling power behind the delicate softness. "You're very sweet," he said quietly, stepping back.

Her eyes flew open. "And *you're* very presumptuous!" she retorted, swiftly turning her back on him to give herself a chance to recover. Just who did he think he was, to awaken feelings she'd thought were buried safely? She adopted a businesslike tone. "I admit I find the view moving, but scarcely sufficient grounds for kissing a total stranger. As for the pool," she continued briskly, "please feel free." She gestured toward the water. "To take a swim, that is," she added hastily, kicking herself mentally for phrasing the invitation so awkwardly. "I was just going to have a quick dip myself," she went on bravely. "I hope you don't mind cold water."

She dove in expertly, swam rapidly to the shallow end, and surfaced, her teeth chattering a little. She was about to head back into deep water in an attempt to warm up when she noticed that he had calmly stripped down to his briefs—which were very brief indeed. "Uh..." She tried clearing her throat. He glanced up from removing a sock and gave her a quizzical look.

"Wouldn't you like to go inside to change?" She tried to make her voice sound natural, but, judging by the grin on his face, she wasn't succeeding. She noticed the well-defined plane of his firm, flat abdominal muscles as they disappeared below the waistband of his briefs. His chest muscles were as well developed as his biceps. As she admired the strong contours of his body, in spite of herself, she felt the cool distance she had created between them dissolve again in the disturbing, churning caldron of her emotions.

"No, thank you," he replied politely. "I didn't bring a bathing suit, you see. I rarely wear one, in fact. But, if you like, I will keep my underwear on. Do I make you uncomfortable, signora?"

Two could play this innocent game, Jennifer decided. "Not at all," she answered stiffly, climbing up the steps at the shallow end as naturally as she could. "I was just going in anyway. Please, make yourself completely at home." She picked up her satchel and cursed herself for having left the cover-up on the terrace. Trying to be as dignified as possible, she walked back toward the villa. Laughter followed her, and then she heard a splash. "I hope he catches pneumonia!" she muttered.

chapter 2

A LONG, LUXURIOUS bubble bath in the huge sunken marble tub in the bathroom adjoining her suite did a lot to ease Jennifer's rattled nerves. She tried to tell herself that her new state of heightened awareness, of excited anticipation, was entirely due to her new job in the magnificent villa. But deep down she could not deny that the moist velvet feel of the stranger's lips on hers had something to do with the way she felt.

She hummed lightly to herself as she toweled off her firm, tingling body with a cloud-soft, deep-lavender bath towel, then wrapped herself in a satiny black floor-length dressing gown, the one splurge her tight budget allowed her for this assignment in Italy. Her feet sank into the deep pile of the rug as she crossed from the bathroom to the nightstand beside

her bed, where she quickly set about brewing a cup
of herbal tea in the little china plug-in pot she'd had
since her college days. With a spoonful of honey, the
tea was just what she needed to relax her so she could
catch a few hours of sleep before dinner that evening.
Tonight she would meet her new colleagues, and she
wanted to be fully rested and as free of the strain of
the past year as possible.

Removing the dressing gown, she slipped naked
between the cool sheets and propped herself up on a
pile of pillows. The soft sheets rubbed against the
tender nipples of her breasts, and she flushed, remembering the way the dark stranger had twirled her
hair and the excitement of having his hand so teasingly
close to her flesh. She sipped her tea, then lay down,
her eyelids heavy. The last thing on her mind as she
eased into sleep was a pair of penetrating ice-blue
eyes.

At the sound of her alarm, Jennifer sat up quickly.
Surely it wasn't time to get up—not yet, not when
she'd found the blissful sleep she'd been seeking for
so long. But a glance at her travel clock assured her
it was getting late.

As she sat before the old-fashioned dressing table
in her bedroom, once more wrapped in her sleek black
dressing gown, Jennifer carefully darkened her long,
full eyelashes with mascara, tied a ribbon around her
head to keep her hair, which varied in color from
wheat to goldenrod, off her face, and applied a touch
of lip gloss. A healthy, well-scrubbed image looked
back at her from the mirror. The chin was firm and
determined, the mouth generous and mobile, the nose
short and straight, and the cheekbones high and lightly

dusted with freckles. Her eyes were large and widely spaced, their color shifting from gray to green. Just now they were gray—and vaguely dissatisfied.

Jennifer made a face at her reflection. "You'll never be glamorous, my dear," she said softly. But that was okay. She rose and went to slip on the colorful cotton print dress she was planning to wear to dinner, then reached under the large four-poster bed in search of her green sandals. After a final look in the mirror, she took a deep breath and walked quickly to the stairs.

She had already explored the villa and knew it to be a vast, rambling structure, to which numerous renovations and additions had been made over the centuries. One wing, occupied by the Hastings School, faced away from the city and looked out over vineyards, orchards, and the Tuscan countryside. The other two single teachers had suites like hers, and Dr. and Mrs. Hastings—and their three lively children—lived in a roomy separate apartment. On the third floor, under the eaves, two comfortable dorm rooms had been set up for the twelve young students who would arrive the following week.

Jennifer wondered briefly about Kurt Sandor, the European businessman who owned the entire estate and kept the other wing of the villa for his private use. She knew that the Hastings were pleased at the interest he took in their school for "difficult" children—and grateful for his gift of the facilities.

Reaching the bottom of the broad flight of stone stairs, Jennifer smiled brightly to see Sam and Marge Hastings already sitting in the gracious common room that looked out onto the terrace. Her pace picked up, and she felt a sudden surge of joy—how wonderful to be together again with her oldest, dearest friends!

At the sound of her footsteps, Marge looked up. "Jen, darling, how great to see you!" she exclaimed, rushing to give her a hug and a kiss. "I hope you haven't been too terribly lonely! You remember Christopher and Nicholas and Matthew?" She gestured vaguely toward three small bodies who were wrestling like puppies out on the terrace. "Of course, they *are* growing fast—can you believe how big they are now? It seems like just yesterday that you were one of Sam's students and we all spent the summer in that tiny apartment downtown in Rome."

Jennifer smiled as Sam came over to give her a big bear hug. "We're both so glad you could join us, Jennifer," he said quietly, "though, naturally, we're sorry for the difficult time you've been going through. We heard about the divorce."

"Thanks for the sentiment, Sam," she said as she felt her eyes filling, "but I think it was a good thing— no, I *know* it was a good thing—so there's really nothing to be sorry about."

He hugged her again, then gave each of them a glass of sherry. "Work is the best therapy, you know," he continued, then raised his glass. "So here's a toast to the summer and to a glorious new chapter in the life of Jennifer Denning."

"And the Hastings School," Jennifer added, a feeling of warmth and security washing over her.

She tossed her blond hair in a gesture of determination and hard-won confidence. Coming here *had* been a good idea—Sam and Marge were right. She looked with love at the couple who had helped her so much, and she had to admit a twinge of jealousy. They were so obviously happy together, so sure of each other's love. There was no bickering, no harsh criticism. Again tears burned at the back of her eyes, but this time they weren't tears of joy, but a reaction to the memory of her marriage to Jeff.

Sam's voice brought her back to the present. "Do you believe it, Marge?" he was asking, pride evident in his tone. "This is the student who thought she'd never manage to keep body and soul together long enough to get her bachelor's degree, let alone a master's! And here she is, *teaching* under me now. Boy, do I feel old." He gave a hearty laugh.

Jennifer studied the rich amber liquid in her glass. "I know how disappointed you were when I wasn't able to go into teaching right away—after all the support both of you gave me to get through college." Marge clucked sympathetically. "But I also know you understood the reasons, that I needed to take a better-paying job, that I had to help Jeff..."

"Of course we understood," Sam said. "And we couldn't be happier that you're going full steam into teaching now, because we need all the help we can get!" He smiled warmly. "Tell us about your arrival, Jen. Are you comfortable?"

Jennifer returned his smile. "Well," she joked, "this place certainly beats my old walk-up—and even the high-rise that Jeff and I later managed to get into. And I've had a lovely peaceful time here by myself—well, almost by myself—relaxing and recovering from jet lag."

"Almost by yourself?" Marge inquired. "Did Don or Vanessa arrive early, too?"

"No, no. I just happened to run into one of the workmen this afternoon, that's all. He stopped here to say they were on the property."

Marge looked concerned. "Did he bother you? If so, we'll have to speak with someone. You shouldn't be subjected—"

"No, no, not at all," Jennifer said quickly. Though the handsome stranger had definitely upset her equilibrium, she didn't want to get him into trouble. She hoped that Marge and Sam would attribute the flush on her cheeks to the sherry.

"Tell me about the other teachers," Jennifer suggested. "I'm looking forward to meeting them."

"Well, first there's Don Allison," Marge began, delighted to share the information. "He's a very nice young man from the Midwest. His specialties are science and math, and he'll also be in charge of physical activities—sports and things."

"And I'm in charge of art appreciation and languages," Jennifer added. "And that leaves—"

"Vanessa Ballard," answered a low, husky voice from the doorway. "Hello, Sam, Marjorie. And you must be Jennifer Denning." She extended her hand, her manner gracious but cool. "It's *so* nice to meet you. I'm the English teacher, to answer your question. But my real specialty is educational therapies—you know, learning disabilities and so forth?" Her tone implied that Jennifer might not understand.

"Of course," Jennifer replied crisply. "I have a degree in special education myself, so I'm acquainted with the field." She smiled stiffly. It would be nice if they all got along, she thought, giving her colleague a long look. Vanessa Ballard was an extremely beautiful woman of about thirty. She had black hair, cut in a short, chic style, and small, perfect features. Her dark eyes were framed by brows with an upward twist, giving her a slightly superior, amused look. She wore diamond studs in her small shell-shaped ears, and her long nails were perfectly manicured. She was wearing trousers and a jade silk tunic, cut at just the right proportion to make her look taller than she was. In short, she was the picture of ultimate sophistication—a sophistication that Jennifer, much to Jeff's displeasure, had never been able to achieve.

Just then the last member of the team arrived. Don Allison had light brown hair that kept falling into his blue eyes, and a pleasant, open face. Jennifer couldn't help but think that his eyes seemed pale in comparison to her stranger's penetrating blue gaze. But Don had the open attitude of the Midwesterner, and Jennifer liked him instinctively.

As Jennifer's attention returned to the group, Maria, the cook, appeared at the doorway to announce dinner, and the group moved in to the dining room.

Everyone was struck by the beauty of the room. "It's just stunning," Vanessa said in a breathy voice. She turned to Marge. "How in the world did you convince the Sandors to give this lovely building to the school?"

Marge smiled at her husband. "Sam's success in working with children who needed a lot of extra attention to keep up with their peers is what did it. As a matter of fact, the Sandors contacted *us*. They'd heard about our program from the parents of one of our ex-pupils, and it seems that the rest just fell into place."

"They've even given the financial backing for the construction needed to house the twenty-five or so students we expect for a full term starting in September," Sam added.

The level of enthusiasm in the room was high, and became even more so when Vanessa asked, "Can anyone tell me about the soiree planned for tomorrow night? The notice on the bulletin board just says, 'Save Saturday evening for a gathering of friends and neighbors.' Are we throwing a party for ourselves?"

"Not really," Marge said eagerly. "The Sandors have invited some people they feel might be interested in our setup here. We'll be having dinner with a few guests, and then a number of other people will arrive afterward. Actually, Mr. Sandor has asked all of us to join him for coffee now, just to go over the details. Oh, and the architect who designed the student cottages will be with him." She smiled, and the group rose to walk toward the doors leading to the terrace.

Marge and Jennifer fell behind the others. "You know, Jen," Marge commented in a serious voice, "if you want to say anything about that workman, now may be the perfect time, with the architect here. I believe he's supervising the work, and he should really know about any problems right away."

Jennifer shook her head. "No, Marge, it's fine— really." She smiled. "Don't worry. After Jeff, I can handle any man."

They stepped out onto the terrace, where Sam, Don, and Vanessa hid Kurt Sandor and the architect from view. Marge took Jennifer by the arm, and they broke into the small circle, laughing. But the sound died on Jennifer's lips. For next to the distinguished, older man, who must be Kurt Sandor, stood an impeccably dressed man whose navy blazer set off his mocking, ice-blue eyes to perfection.

chapter 3

"ARE YOU OKAY, hon?" Marge's voice was full of concern. Aware that the entire group was staring at her, Jennifer tried to gather her wits.

"Y-yes," she stammered. "I think my shoe must have gotten caught on one of the stones."

Kurt Sandor was instantly solicitous, but the tall, muscular man to his right moved faster. "Signora," he said, taking her arm, "you must be very careful. In Italy, and particularly in Florence, we don't like to see any treasures damaged." His voice was smooth, comforting—and full of baloney, Jennifer thought to herself. She also noticed that he now spoke fluent classical Italian, that all traces of the local dialect and accent were gone. What a rat, leading her along like that!

She grabbed back her arm, not caring that the gesture must seem rude to the others, and forced her gaze to meet his. "I'm sure you're referring only to *authentic* treasures," she responded in her very best Italian. "Not the fakes."

If she expected him to be chastised by her remark and put in his place, she was wrong. Undaunted, he took her right hand and moved it toward his lips, pausing to hold it mere inches away. He spoke again, his tantalizing breath caressing her skin. "I wasn't aware of any fakes in Florence," he said. "At least not of any Italian ones. Perhaps the signora is speaking about the work of *foreign* artists...If so, I would certainly appreciate your instruction, signora," he finished, then grazed her hand with his lips.

"Well," Sam broke in heartily, dispelling the others' curious expressions, "now that you two have met, I'd like to introduce Kurt Sandor to you, Jennifer. As you've just seen, Kurt, Mrs. Denning speaks perfect Italian, something I never managed to do."

Still blazing under the architect's scrutiny, Jennifer turned to Kurt Sandor. "How do you do," she said, this time in English. Did the other man speak it at all, she wondered? He must. And she still didn't know his name.

She'd show him that he wasn't the only smooth operator around. "And I must thank Signor... Signor... for helping me," she smiled sweetly at Kurt Sandor and gestured gracefully in the architect's direction.

"Please forgive us, Mrs. Denning," he said. "This is Signor DiRenzo."

She turned to him, extending her hand. "Charmed,"

she said to him. She hoped the irony in that one word would not escape him. She was sure little did.

Excusing herself from the group a few minutes later, she walked over to the edge of the terrace nearest the pool and peered through the trees to see if she could catch a better view of Florence spread out below, made crimson by the setting sun.

"You can see it quite well from the second floor," said a now-familiar voice in Italian. She jumped. "Did I startle you, signora?"

"As a matter of fact, you did," she replied, "though you'd think I'd be accustomed to your style of approach by now."

She turned to see that he held out an exquisite, tiny cup filled with espresso. *"Grazie tanto,"* she murmured as she took it. His hand grazed hers.

Suddenly she felt very uncomfortable. She gestured in the direction of their host, who stood talking with the others.

"Have you known Mr. Sandor long?" she asked.

"Yes," he replied. "In fact, I've known both him and his wife for several years. I believe we met in Rome—yes, that's right." He grinned broadly, and Jennifer couldn't help but admire the crinkly corners around his bright eyes. But she was determined to ignore his lightly veiled reference to their earlier conversation.

"I know you share my passion for the view from the pool, Signor DiRenzo," she continued, pretending not to be aware that he had moved even closer to her or that the heady maleness of his scent was carried to her on the gentle breeze. "I'm sure you agree that the entire estate is simply magnificent. It's a privilege to be here."

"Ah, yes," he said. "Beauty is very important to us Italians. And when we find we don't have enough of it, we take care to import it." In a deft motion, he swept her long hair off the back of her neck, and she thrilled to the series of light, feathery kisses he ran along it. Despite an inner voice that warned her he was being too forward, she was lost in the moment— until Vanessa's voice broke into her reverie.

"Come on, you two," she called out. "We're going to discuss the party." Thank goodness for the twilight, Jennifer thought as she and DiRenzo moved toward the others, his hand at the small of her back. Or maybe Vanessa *had* seen what was going on between them . . .

"So, after dinner in the dining room, we will adjourn to the ballroom for dancing," Kurt Sandor was saying. "There will be an orchestra, of course, and a late buffet set up in the drawing room. I expect about one hundred fifty people altogether, though, as I said, we will be just twenty for dinner."

Jennifer moved away from DiRenzo to perch on the arm of Sam's chair. She realized that the gesture was almost one of defiance to DiRenzo and meant a return to safety for her. She took further refuge in studying Kurt Sandor. His eyes were dark and veiled, but she couldn't tell whether his expression was caused by the evening shadows or whether he was secretive. His face was lined, but his main concession to age—Jennifer knew he must be in his fifties—was his perfectly cut, slightly thinning silver hair. He

looked very sophisticated and terribly European—
without DiRenzo's rakish touch, she decided.

She felt DiRenzo's burning gaze on her and forced
herself to pay more attention to Mr. Sandor. "I must
tell you how pleased I am to have all of you here at
the villa," he continued. "As you are no doubt aware,
I am not in residence for much of the year, and this
is only my wife's second visit. Incidentally, she begs
to be excused tonight. She is resting from the trip. I
am glad that the estate will be put to such good use
in the coming year, and I look forward to a long and
happy collaboration among us all." Jennifer half-ex-
pected him to click his heels; his bearing was so formal
as to be almost military. "And now, may I offer anyone another espresso? Or some cognac? Let us enjoy
this fine evening and get acquainted."

As Vanessa instantly took advantage of Kurt Sandor's invitation, DiRenzo came over to Marge and
Jennifer. He shook Marge's hand, then held Jennifer's
for a second longer than was necessary. He was, to
all appearances, the perfect gentleman. "Until tomorrow evening, signora," he said, then turned to
take his leave of the others.

"Wow!" Marge exclaimed. "That's some man."

"You're right about that," Jennifer agreed, and saw
that the irony of her tone was completely lost on
Marge, who was hellbent on seeing Jennifer "settle
down" again. Jennifer nodded toward their host. "Mr.
Sandor isn't so bad either, Marge," she pointed out,
"and he seems to be every inch the gentleman. So
cultured, so polite, so gracious..."

"And so *rich,*" Don Allison added in a whisper,

joining the two women. "And it's pretty clear that Vanessa knows the score. But then, this place is incredible! And it's only *one* of his houses—the one he visits only a few times a year! Gosh! Where does the man actually live?"

"Mostly in Switzerland," Marge answered. "The Sandors have an apartment in Zurich and a ski chalet in Gstaad."

"Tsk, tsk," Don mocked. "Well, that's sensible, what with secret Swiss bank accounts and all..."

"Well, *I* think he's very nice," Jennifer said seriously. "As I understand it, he's a self-made man, so he deserves everything he's got. And look what he's giving us..." Her voice trailed off as their host strolled over to them. "I'm sure it will be a lovely party, Mr. Sandor," she said. "We're all looking forward to it."

"Please, it would do me a great honor if you would call me Kurt." His comment embraced the threesome, but his insistent eyes were on Jennifer. "After all, we are close neighbors, are we not? Practically family."

"And we hope to become good friends," Marge said warmly. "You've been very kind, Kurt, but since my kids are bound to wake me at the crack of dawn, I think I'll turn in. Sam?" she called.

Jennifer, too, held out her hand to Sandor to say goodnight.

"I have some beautiful pieces in the villa, Jennifer," he said, kissing the back of her hand in a courtly fashion, "and I hope to be able to show you some of them sometime. I know that you have both interest and expertise in art."

"I'd love to see the collection," she replied sincerely. "Good night."

"Buona sera."

Feeling tired from the wine and the excitement, Jennifer walked slowly up the stairs to her room. After having removed her makeup, she slid once more between the cool, welcoming sheets. For the second time that day, the last thing on her mind before she slept was a pair of mocking, playful—and enticing—blue eyes.

chapter 4

SURVEYING HER FEW DRESSES, which seemed even fewer due to the large, opulent armoire that housed them, Jennifer sighed. "Well, the surroundings may be ritzy, kid," she said to herself, "but unfortunately, you're not." Just that day she'd gazed with longing into the chic shop windows along Florence's Via Tornabuoni as she acquainted herself with the city. At the moment, however, the thought of those designer clothes only served to remind her of her low bank account. Thank heavens that Florence's art treasures could be seen for nothing, since that was about all she could afford to pay!

What in the world would she wear tonight to the dance? Her eye fell on the rich material of the black dressing gown—her one luxury—and for an instant she regretted spending so much on it, rather than getting a good dress for evening wear.

Suddenly she had an idea. Perhaps she could re-create a dress she had seen in a shop window that afternoon . . . if she dared. Opening the bureau where her underwear lay folded in neat piles, she drew out a white cotton camisole trimmed with eyelet embroidery and blue ribbon and a long half-slip with a matching ruffle around the bottom. She held them up to herself and looked critically in the mirror. If she took her wide blue satin hair ribbon and used it as a sash, the outfit would be just like one she'd seen in the window of an expensive boutique. Her smile widened. With any luck, everyone would think she was very fashionable—not that she was wearing lingerie!

To add to her dressy appearance, Jennifer put her golden hair up in a soft knot at the top of her head, allowing a few tendrils to escape around her face and at the nape of her neck. A touch of jade eyeliner—to bring out the green of her eyes—and lots of brown mascara, completed the look. She didn't need any blusher. The combination of eagerness and dread with which she viewed the night's proceedings gave her cheeks plenty of color.

DiRenzo would be there, full of Old World charm . . . and wiles. How would her outfit fare under his critical gaze? She chased the consideration from her mind. She'd never met Jeff's standards or his family's, and she refused to subject herself to that kind of criticism again. Let Vanessa be the fashion plate of the evening.

After a spray of cologne and a touch of lipstick, Jennifer stepped into the hallway, and into Don's path. Looking young and well-scrubbed in a double-breasted navy blazer and white trousers, he gave a cheerful whistle of appreciation. Jennifer's smile deepened. "You look terrific!" he said with enthusiasm.

Her morale considerably bolstered by this first re-action to her appearance, she took his proffered arm and started down the stairs. "Thanks, Don," she said warmly. At that moment Vanessa joined them, stunning in a black halter-neck gown with a plunging neckline and no back at all.

"Good evening," she breathed huskily, floating past them on a cloud of My Sin. "You look simply charming together. Are they serving cocktails on the terrace?" Without waiting for an answer, she drifted through the doors.

Jennifer noted that Don had been made speechless by Vanessa's appearance. So much for raiding underwear drawers, she thought wryly. She tapped his shoulder good-naturedly to get his attention. "Heads up," she remarked lightly, "or we'll go flying down these stairs."

"Sorry, Jennifer," he replied sheepishly as they reached the main floor. "Can I get you a drink? It's...uh...just that I hadn't seen...so much...of Vanessa before. And she *is* an eyeful in that dress." He laughed. "Now, what can I get you?"

"*Cinzano bianco,* please." Jennifer surveyed the terrace as Don left her side. Festooned with tiny white lights and illuminated by big, fat candles on tall, sturdy standards, it looked like a fairyland. Then she saw him. At least *some* men didn't seem to be made speechless by Vanessa's charms, she noted. Quite the opposite. For the dark-haired woman now stood between Kurt Sandor and Signor DiRenzo at the far end of the terrace, carrying on an animated conversation. For some reason, Jennifer's heart sank as the tall architect laughed appreciatively at one of the pretty brunette's comments and ran his eyes over her sleek, sophisticated form with obvious admiration.

There's more than one fish in the sea, Jennifer reflected, and Signor DiRenzo apparently took an interest in them all. At that moment, he looked her way and raised his glass in greeting. It was just like the man to catch her staring at him, she thought. Her embarrassment was only increased by the appearance of Marge Hastings at her side.

"I was wondering where you were," she exclaimed, taking Jennifer firmly by the elbow. Once close, she whispered conspiratorially, "This assignment might do you more good than either Sam or I thought. I'm sure our architect friend has got his eye on you!"

"But isn't he married?" Jennifer asked, appalled to learn that his interest was so obvious.

"Not that I know of. Whatever gave you that idea?" Ignoring Jennifer's look of surprise, Marge continued in a normal voice, "You look simply enchanting, Jen, and so chic. All the fashion magazines at the beauty parlor today had pictures of models wearing what looked to me like petticoats. Some of them looked as if they hadn't dressed yet, but on you it looks great! Now, where's your drink? There! Thanks, Don—let's mingle. I have dozens of people I want you to meet." Jennifer allowed Marge to introduce a number of the distinguished guests to her, and was impressed by the range of Kurt Sandor's friendships. Yet no matter how intriguing each new acquaintance was, Jennifer found her eyes drawn to whatever corner of the terrace Sig-

nor DiRenzo occupied. She was furious that he had
let her think he was married. And all that talk about
bambini! He had let her make a complete fool of
herself in more ways than one.

Yet, as the evening progressed, he seemed intensely aware of her as well—so much so that she
almost felt as if they were each equipped with some
kind of internal compass that kept a constant watch
for the other's presence. They seemed to circle each
other warily around the terrace, and Jennifer felt the
very air crackle with tension. A flood of relief washed
over her when dinner was announced.

Her relief did not last long. *"Permesso?"* a velvet
voice asked as a firm arm slipped around her waist.
Somehow what should have been a request sounded
like a command.

Having done well up to this point in their battle of
nerves, Jennifer wasn't about to admit defeat now.
"Con gusto," she replied smoothly, although she
didn't actually feel much pleasure at the thought of
having to dine next to him. But she did have to admit
he looked particularly handsome, his white dinner
jacket, snowy formal shirt, and black tie setting off
his angular, tanned face to perfection. His light blue
eyes seemed to blaze in the twilight.

"How very nice to see you again, Signora Denning," he said, again giving the word "signora" an
infuriating twist.

He was teasing her because she had made such a
point of her marital status. By now, of course, someone must have told him she was divorced. If he had
bothered to ask.

"Did you have a pleasant swim yesterday?" she

inquired. Disregarding his mild baiting was probably the best way to handle it.

"Not so pleasant as it might have been had you stayed," he replied, smiling wickedly.

Jennifer was about to retort when they swept into the dining room. Unbelievably the room was even more magnificent than the one in the school wing. The ceiling was easily eighteen feet high, and the walls were covered with heavy moiré silk. The silver on the huge refectory table was massive and heavy— probably Renaissance, Jennifer conjectured—and the china was Limoges.

"Stunning, isn't it?" Signor DiRenzo commented, as if reading her thoughts. "One would probably have to travel far, at least as far as, say...Rome, to find a room of equal beauty." The glinting eyes were full of mischief.

Immediately she was angry. All right, so she'd made a mistake in assuming he was one of the construction workers. But he certainly hadn't said anything to set her straight. She'd put an end to his harping on her comments about Rome, and right now.

As casually as possible, she took a side step and brought her heel down firmly on his foot. Her only regret was that she wasn't wearing spiked heels.

"Oh, do forgive me!" she cooed as he grimaced slightly, then quickly recovered. She had to admit that he handled himself well. "It's amazing the amount of self-control the artists who constructed this room must have demonstrated throughout their careers," she commented.

"Hmm...," he mused. "It makes one think about those fakes you mentioned earlier. I'm sure *their* careers showed remarkably little restraint." Though he smiled, the pressure on her arm increased.

She deserved that one, she knew—though she'd die before admitting it. She checked coolly for her assigned seat. To her surprise, she was to dine at Kurt Sandor's left. She had expected to be much farther down the table. As DiRenzo slipped casually into the chair next to her, between her and Vanessa, Jennifer sighed and turned her attention to the opposite side of the table, where Alicia Sandor sat. A small, vivacious woman, each of her blond hairs in perfect place, she wore a spectacular beaded gown that sparkled in the candlelight. She smiled frequently and participated in the flow of conversation around her.

As did Vanessa, Jennifer realized, noticing that her colleague was delighting DiRenzo with her slightly fumbling Italian. She was probably just the kind of woman who would appeal to the mesmerizing Signor DiRenzo, Jennifer thought—worldly, sophisticated, chic. It was just as well, she told herself firmly, willing the tension inside her to calm down with little success. Vanessa and DiRenzo would make a perfect couple, and she would no longer have to deal with the range of troubling emotions he seemed capable of generating in her.

"Don't you like the consommé?" Kurt Sandor asked gently.

With a start Jennifer realized that everyone else had already begun on the soup course. "Daydreaming?" he teased. Smiling paternally, he turned back to the woman on his other side. Her dining partners occupied, Jennifer studied the room. Funny how she still felt uneasy in elegant surroundings. A legacy from her experiences with Jeff and his family, she thought, remembering the uncomfortable meals she'd eaten in her in-laws' gracious home in a wealthy suburb of New York City.

Her mother-in-law had had more concern for her crystal and china than for Jennifer's feelings. She constantly brought up the names of friends' daughters, young women who had gone into the traditional men's fields—law, engineering, medicine. Jennifer's teaching position didn't bring Mrs. Denning enough status in the eyes of her friends. Apparently, Mrs. Denning didn't care that Jennifer's "women's work" was financing Jeff's education. Of course, it wasn't until later that Jennifer learned that neither of Jeff's parents even knew that she was supporting him—he had told them he'd been awarded a prestigious scholarship. She clenched her hands at the memory. With all their money, you'd think they could have been generous— not just financially, but emotionally as well. And Jeff, she had realized in the course of their marriage, was just as selfish and determinedly upwardly mobile as they were.

DiRenzo's voice broke into Jennifer's thoughts. "It's strange, is it not, how this room combines the rough with the smooth—expected, almost stale elements with ones that are vital and new." His tone was urgent, as if he were trying to comment on more than just the design of the room. "Some pieces are definitely medieval. This table, for instance, is from a twelfth-century monastery—and therefore almost Primitive. Some pieces are very refined—the Viennese crystal chandelier, the china, the wall-covering. I adore contradictions," he continued, his voice lower, deeper. "The tension they create is, I think, exciting."

"That's an interesting point of view, signor," she acknowledged, "but I'm sure many people feel that there isn't enough harmony in their lives."

He raised his eyebrows. "Perhaps the signora has just such a need for harmony?"

She refused to answer, and when the soup was followed by extremely thin pasta tossed in a cream sauce with peas and bits of prosciutto, DiRenzo became an efficient tourist guide.

"That's called *capelli d'angeli*—angel's hair," he explained, translating the name into a softly accented English. She looked up from her plate with interest. Did he speak English after all? "You will also frequently find green spinach noodles mixed with the plain ones in a similar preparation," he continued in Italian, "and that's called *paglia e fieno*—straw and hay." His tone was genial, not overbearing.

"I know," she replied calmly. "Though I appreciate the refresher course, I have lived in Italy before, signor."

He seemed oblivious to her implied rebuke and smiled engagingly. "I *knew* it," he announced triumphantly. "I knew your Italian was too good to have been acquired exclusively in a classroom! Where were you? Here in Florence?"

"No, in Rome." She flushed slightly, and his eyes twinkled. "It was several years ago," she added, ignoring her embarrassment and wondering where *he* had been that summer, before she had married Jeff. Was he studying in Bologna, perhaps? It suddenly seemed terribly important to know all about this enigmatic man, but just as she was going to ask him where he grew up, Vanessa tapped him on the shoulder, and his head inclined in the other direction. Jennifer bit her tongue, fighting unexpected disappointment.

She turned her attention to their host while the rest of the meal—a roast saddle of veal, lightly cooked vegetables, and salad—was served, all the time intensely aware of DiRenzo's presence. Finally, after most of the guests had served themselves from generous platters of fresh fruit and cheeses, Jennifer tried to sneak a look at him. He noticed immediately.

"The signora does not care for any fruit?" he asked, his tone innocent but his eyes full of mischief. With that remark he deftly peeled an apple with a knife and fork, then skillfully sliced it, and put one piece in his mouth. "Mmm," he savored. "Perhaps the signora would like me to..." He moved his knife and fork toward the apple resting on her plate in the manner of someone who was going to cut something for a child.

She placed a restraining hand swiftly on his wrist, thinking for only a second about the warmth that coursed through her fingertips, at the feathery touch of the dark, manly hairs against her smooth skin. "I can handle this, thank you, signor," she said. Yet when she tried to imitate his skillful action, the apple bounced off her plate and would have landed on the floor had he not caught it with one hand in a lightning-fast motion. Mortified, Jennifer wished it *had* rolled under the table. Then, at least, she could have followed it there and not have had to face DiRenzo's eyes, which were now practically dancing with laughter.

Before he could say anything, Kurt Sandor rose

and tapped his wineglass lightly with a knife to gain the attention of the diners. Jennifer turned to look at him, but all she could think of was DiRenzo on the other side of her, delighting in her discomfort. "Honored guests," their host began, "I believe I hear the strains of the orchestra tuning up, so let's adjourn to the ballroom." To Jennifer's surprise and relief, he turned to her and offered her his arm. "May I have the pleasure?" he asked.

"Of course," she agreed warmly, grateful for the chance to escape DiRenzo.

But if she thought she could escape him so easily, she was mistaken. At the end of every dance, and often as she was being whirled around the room, their eyes met. No longer mocking, his gaze now held a more serious, ardent look—one of *desire*. For a long time now whenever men looked at her that way she had warned them off with a sarcastic tongue and a fierce dedication to her work. Never again would she let a man do to her what Jeff had done—destroy her self-confidence and make her feel undesirable.

Yet there was no stopping DiRenzo, she thought suddenly, a thrill running through her. With a start, she realized that the thrill was one of longing rather than fear.

At that moment he appeared beside her, just as the orchestra began playing music for a slow dance. Without asking permission, he took her in his arms, not as the other men she'd danced with had, with their light, friendly touches, but as if he were certain they belonged together. He drew her close, so close that she felt overwhelmed by his presence. Through the flimsy material of the camisole, the tips of her breasts touched his firm, muscled chest, and the slow, burning warmth in the pit of her stomach turned rapidly into a fire that spread out to her fingertips. Her cheek felt hot against his shoulder. *"Sei molto bella stasera,"* he whispered—"You're very beautiful this evening"— and she felt herself melting. She noticed that he used the intimate, familiar form of address.

He was calling up feelings in her she wasn't sure she could handle, emotions that threatened to take over her very being. But somehow, at that moment, all that mattered was being in his arms. The music stopped, and without a word he led her out to the deserted terrace. The sky was now a brilliant canopy of deep black velvet sprinkled with thousands upon thousands of glimmering stars. Abandoning all cares, she leaned her head against his steady shoulder, finding refuge in his strong embrace. She noticed nothing but the pleasant scent of candle wax mingled with the heady sweetness of moonflowers, in full bloom on a vine that climbed the side of the villa, and the comforting rhythm of his breathing, of their breathing together. The gentle evening air caressed them.

His hand moved up and down her slender neck, making the wispy tendrils of hair rise and fall. Despite her excitement, Jennifer felt an ages-old calm inside, a feeling that this man, this place, were somehow right, something she'd been destined for. She felt like a woman again.

Gently he took her face in his two hands and gazed for a long time into her eyes. Then he kissed her, first with the velvet-soft touch of yesterday morning, then with a growing insistence as she responded. His probing tongue parted her lips and found the moist warmth within. He pressed more firmly against her, ever seeking, and she thought she would swoon with pleasure. Jeff had never aroused such feelings in her. And this was only a kiss, for heaven's sake!

DiRenzo moved one arm behind her back to support her as she arched to receive his kiss. The other hand moved over her right breast and teased her nipple with a slow circular motion. She gasped in delight. He settled her down on the low stone wall surrounding the terrace, his kisses growing ever more demanding, his caressing fingers exciting her to a fever pitch. Before she knew what she was doing, she had placed a hand on his chest and started to unbutton his shirt. Her fingers slipped inside.

"Cara," he groaned. *"Cara mia . . ."*—"My precious one." With a deft motion he loosened her hair, which came cascading down around them. *"Cara,* I must have you," he murmured. "I'm staying just down the road in a cottage. Come with me . . ." He ran kisses down her neck, pausing at the hollow of her throat. As he moved down to the swell of her breasts, the exact meaning of his words finally registered. A tremor of fear shot through her and some part of her deep inside stiffened in resistance. How dare he just assume she would tumble into bed with him, a perfect stranger! What conceited arrogance! Summoning all her willpower, she pulled firmly away from him.

"How dare you suggest such a thing. We hardly know each other," she protested, ignoring the sudden thought that that hadn't bothered her until now. "I don't even know your first name!" She realized that the world had changed while she'd been married, but she had her own standards to maintain.

DiRenzo laughed softly, and she was glad it was too dark to see his eyes. "But I thought you were a liberated American woman!" he commented, still amused. "A divorcée, no less. And surely we want the same thing..."

Furious at his insinuations, Jennifer made no reply, merely rose stiffly and hurried across the terrace toward the welcome light of the ballroom. So all men *were* the same, she thought bitterly. They all wanted one thing—and one thing only.

"Getting some air?" Vanessa drawled as she stepped through the french doors. "Or just discussing architectural theory and some of the finer points of the villa's construction?"

"Neither, really, Vanessa," Jennifer replied curtly. "Though *my* Italian is quite good, Signor DiRenzo and I can't find a common language." She hurried past her to the powder room, where she quickly redid her hair and splashed cool water on her flushed cheeks. After a few minutes, she felt able to face the crowd again.

To her relief, Kurt Sandor saw her as she stepped back into the ballroom, and in his courtly fashion he begged for the honor of dancing with her. She found refuge in his fatherly arms. He left space between their bodies—unlike DiRenzo—so it was easy to talk.

"Have you been enjoying yourself since dinner?" he asked as he guided her expertly across the floor.

"I've been having a wonderful time," she replied sincerely. Until ten minutes ago, she added silently. "Meeting your guests and dancing is so wonderful. It's such a treat to hear such a fine orchestra"—even to have one at all, she acknowledged to herself. "This is a magical evening."

A serious look came onto Kurt Sandor's face. "I understand from Dr. and Mrs. Hastings that you are recently divorced, Jennifer. I know it's not an easy subject to talk about, but may I ask if you were married for long?"

"Of course you may." Though it was a painful topic to discuss, she felt the need to speak with someone, and she found Kurt Sandor a sympathetic listener. His calm, undemanding presence was a relief after the highly charged scene with DiRenzo. "I was married for nearly six years. We were too young, I guess, and we grew into two very different people." She didn't go into their financial problems, Jeff's criticism of her unsophisticated ways, his dependence on her for money to put him through medical school, or the pain he'd caused her when he left her for another woman. She gave an involuntary shudder as she remembered what a stranger Jeff had become by the end of their marriage, how cold and uncaring he'd been the last time they were together.

"I'm so sorry." Feeling her shiver, Sandor had tightened his grasp. "It must have been difficult. And it was unfeeling of me to bring it up."

"Not at all." Jennifer forced herself to smile. "It's all still quite recent, of course, but I'm beginning to recover. You're very kind to be concerned."

"Thank you for saying so. Incidentally, I wanted to repeat my invitation for a tour of my collection, though, unfortunately, it will have to be postponed for a time."

"Oh?"

"Yes. Tomorrow I must leave to accompany Alicia to Zurich, and then business will keep me away for some time."

"I'm sorry," Jennifer said genuinely disappointed. "I didn't realize you would be leaving so soon. You won't even get to meet our first group of students."

"Not on this visit." He sounded regretful. "I had planned on staying for another week or so, but Alicia finds the climate uncongenial and wishes to return to Switzerland. So..." He shrugged and gave a sad smile.

"That's a shame," Jennifer said. "I do hope she feels better."

"Yes, that would be a blessing." He looked resigned, then seemed to shake off the mood. "I want you to promise me something," he added, the sparkle returning to his eyes. "Promise me a game of tennis when I return. I have just had the court refinished, and I was so looking foward to playing. You look as though you're a strong player. You move beautifully."

"Yes, I *do* play," Jennifer said, pleased, "and I'd love to play with you."

A silence fell between them, and suddenly Jennifer asked, "Do you have children, Kurt?" She blushed furiously when she realized how personal her question sounded—as did the use of his first name. "Forgive me, I don't know what put that in my mind."

"Curiosity, I imagine," he replied easily. "And the answer is no, I have no children. But if I had a daughter, I would want her to be just as sunny and beautiful as you are, Jennifer."

As the music stopped and the band prepared to take a break, Alicia Sandor joined them. She favored Jennifer with a warm smile. "Such a lovely ensemble, my dear," she said sincerely. "You look so fresh. Like a perfect flower." She turned to her husband. "I'm afraid I must retire, Kurt," she said quietly. "I have developed a splitting headache. You will make my excuses?" Without waiting for a reply, she nodded pleasantly at Jennifer and started toward the private wing of the villa. Kurt Sandor watched her leave, his eyes veiled. He looked as though he wanted to go after her.

"Excuse me," Jennifer said softly, taking the opportunity to go up to Sam and Marge, whom she hadn't spoken with since before dinner. "What a marvelous party!" she exclaimed to them.

"And you're the belle of the ball, as far as I can tell," Sam noted. "Dancing with all the gentlemen."

"And one who's *not* a gentleman," Jennifer blurted, her swirling, pent-up emotions released in the company of these close friends. Yes, even as she spoke, she knew her words and voice were overly harsh. Perhaps she was hopelessly old-fashioned as far as DiRenzo was concerned. "I thought Rome and points south had the monopoly on arrogant skirt-chasing Italians, but I was evidently mistaken. Even cultured, northern Italian types have a very macho view of the world."

Marge clucked sympathetically. "I find it hard to believe that one of Kurt's guests was rude, my dear. Tell me, which one is the culprit?" Her shrewd eyes swept the ballroom.

"It's that architect, DiRenzo. I must admit I found him attractive initially, but he's not nearly as irresistible as he seems to think!"

"Stephen?" Sam sounded shocked. "Actually, I'm not at all surprised he made a pass, but he's not Italian, Jen. We spoke a bit yesterday. He has the same last name as a college friend of mine. It turns out that my friend is our architect's uncle. Small world... Stephen has spent a great deal of time abroad, of course, but he was born in New York."

Jennifer was mortified! How could she have made such a stupid assumption? And how could he have permitted her to go on, always speaking Italian. Her cheeks went crimson. "I... I... just assumed he was Italian," she stammered. "When we first met yesterday, he addressed me in Italian, and so naturally I thought... and his name..."

"It was a perfectly understandable mistake, dear," Marge soothed.

But despite her friend's sympathy, or perhaps because of it, Jennifer felt a need to be alone, to get away and think. "I think I'll get a breath of fresh air." She guessed the terrace would be safe by now. Stephen and Vanessa were undoubtedly occupied elsewhere. Outdoors, she took a deep breath, letting the smell of dew-touched grass fill her nostrils. The breeze seemed sharper now, and she shivered.

She'd thought she'd learned her lesson. Why was she always so gullible when it came to men? Gullible—and vulnerable?

"You must be thirsty by now—with all the dancing," said Stephen DiRenzo in Italian, coming up behind her. "Our host had you on the dance floor for quite a while, I noticed. Here, I've brought you a glass of wine."

Jennifer turned abruptly to face him. "I don't need

anything from *you,* Stephen," she replied pointedly
in English. "And now that I've provided your amusement for the weekend, please excuse me!" She moved
to brush past him, but he grasped her by the shoulders,
heedless of her anger.

"What? No sense of humor? Surely such a pretty,
intelligent woman can take a joke! Especially since
you started it." His face was very close to hers, and
she could smell a faint hint of shaving cream and
perspiration, plus an intriguing heathery scent that
seemed to be his alone.

"I can take a joke, *Mr.* DiRenzo," she managed
to say, trying to hold on to her anger as the contagious
look of merriment in his eyes threatened to drive it
away. "But I don't like being laughed at. And I don't
relish the company of arrogant, self-centered men who
enjoy themselves at someone else's expense. Good
night!" She broke free and hurried inside, relieved to
see that the guests were beginning to leave. She was
torn by conflicting emotions—anger with the worldly
Stephen DiRenzo, who was apparently just playing
with her, and a strange, unsettling feeling she refused
to name. Even his brief touch on her shoulder seemed
indelible. She could feel it still, as though his fingers
had burned a permanent impression on her naked skin.

Suddenly she felt very tired. She located Don, who
was standing near the bar, and asked for a glass of
wine. Stephen DiRenzo was right, damn him. She
was thirsty and the wine tasted very good. As she
sipped it with pleasure, Stephen caught her eye from
across the room, where he was standing by the french
doors. Still furious, she turned her back pointedly to
him.

chapter 5

A WEEK LATER, some of the students arrived by car, others by plane or train. A boy named Herbert, who was reputed to be extremely troublesome and disruptive, disembarked from a helicopter in a nearby field. "I suspect we're seeing this kid's major problem right now," Don whispered. "He flies here in a private helicopter with his own pilot and—who's that other character? His valet? Where in the world are his parents?"

Jennifer nodded in agreement as the entourage headed toward the villa. Herbert, she suspected, was going to be a real challenge. Despite his near-genius IQ, he hadn't yet successfully completed a single grade level. She had a gut feeling, though, that if she could just find something that really interested the boy... She shook her head. This job was going to demand everything she had to give.

No sooner had Herbert settled in than Don hopped into the aging Fiat he'd bought recently and headed down into Florence to meet another arrival at the train station. Jennifer paused on the terrace to get her breath. Hearing the sound of tires crunching on the gravel, she lifted her head as a huge Mercedes limousine pulled up by the main entrance. A uniformed chauffeur leaped out of the automobile and moved to open the rear door as Jennifer approached it. "Hello, there," she said, smiling down at one of the most enchanting little girls she'd ever seen. "My name is Jennifer Denning. What's yours?"

She bent over slightly to be at the same level as the child, who gazed at her solemnly with enormous dark eyes that looked like bottomless wells. Perfectly cut, dark brown bangs framed those velvet eyes, and the rest of her hair curved in at her chin in a pageboy. Her face was heart shaped, and she was wearing a beautiful white piqué dress. She reached out calmly and took Jennifer's hand, then climbed gracefully out of the enormous car. She looked around silently. Jennifer was so mesmerized by the child that she scarcely noticed the man who followed her out of the back seat.

"How do you do, Miss Denning?" he said briskly. "I'm Nelson Abbott, and this is my daughter, Mary."

"Forgive me, Mr. Abbott," Jennifer replied, seeing the balding, bespectacled man for the first time. "How rude of me. It's a pleasure to meet you and to welcome you both to the Hastings School."

"It's not rude at all," he responded pleasantly.

"Your first interest seems to be Mary—and that's exactly as it should be."

Jennifer frowned slightly, recalling the records she had studied on Mary Abbott. Good schoolwork, as she remembered, and astonishing reading comprehension scores. But extremely withdrawn. The child had stopped speaking after her mother's death four years ago. Jennifer smiled hopefully. "I'm sure we'll get along famously, Mr. Abbott. And we'll certainly do our best to help Mary."

Nelson Abbott sighed, then gathered his daughter up in his arms. "Good-bye, Pumpkin," he said gently. Jennifer saw a tear roll down one of his cheeks. The child returned his gaze seriously, then wiped the tear away. For a moment, she buried her head in his neck and clung to him, then she drew back and he put her down. She walked over to where Jennifer was standing and took her hand dutifully. When her father's departing car disappeared around the bend, she looked up at Jennifer as if to say, "Now what?"

On impulse, Jennifer started toward the swimming pool. "Come on, Mary," she said eagerly. "From over here we can see the road all the way back down into Florence, so we can follow your Daddy's car as he drives to the city. And you can also see a very beautiful sight." She directed the girl's attention to the winding road that snaked down the hill toward the Arno. They watched the automobile getting smaller and smaller with every bend. And then Jennifer turned the small body, pointing her to watch Florence itself, which shimmered in the sun. She was rewarded with a small gasp and, she thought, just the hint of a smile on Mary's lips.

"Isn't it lovely?" Jennifer said, once again feeling as though the panorama were reaching up and embracing her with its warm brick and ochre colors. "And there are so many beautiful things in that city. And I'm going to show them all to you—every one!" The child's solemn look seemed to hold her to that promise. The warm sun caressed Jennifer's shoulders, and suddenly everything seemed possible. She was filled with confidence and energy. Mary's arm came up abruptly, pointing at a gleaming object near the center of the city.

"That's the Duomo," explained a rich masculine voice behind them. For once Stephen did not startle Jennifer. He seemed to fit perfectly into the scene. Mary didn't seem at all alarmed by his presence. In fact, she seemed to become more calm, more at ease. "It's the largest cathedral in Florence," he went on, "and one of the most spectacular in Italy. You must be sure to have Mrs. Denning take you there on one of your first excursions."

An intent expression on her face, Mary nodded at Stephen. As the two adults turned back toward the villa, Jennifer noted that Mary placed one trusting hand in her own and the other in Stephen's. For a moment, Jennifer allowed herself a flight of fancy, thinking that the three of them could almost pass for a family. A family . . . Jeff had even come to begrudge her the time she'd spent with her students—and had firmly vetoed the idea of having a child of their own.

Stephen's voice, speaking Italian, broke into her thoughts. "You and the little one seem to have a certain understanding," he said to her. "I know Mary's father and I know she doesn't take to new people easily." His melting blue eyes looked down into hers. "This little one has been hurt, and she's protecting herself. I think she senses that you've been hurt, too." He reached over to brush away a lock of golden hair that had fallen across her cheek. Jennifer was shocked to see that all traces of his usual mockery were absent from his expression.

When they reached the villa, Stephen shook Mary's small hand, then Jennifer's, and moved off quietly before she could say a word.

Was this the same man whose hard mouth had taken possession of hers, whose desire had reawakened her own? The same man who had asked her in a husky voice to come with him to his cottage? She realized with a quickening of her pulse that there was much, much more to Stephen DiRenzo than met the eye.

After a week's worth of classes, Jennifer became more attuned to the needs of her students. Herbert definitely was turned off in the classroom. She thought a field trip might be what he needed. Yet as she led the way through one of the magnificent galleries in the Uffizi, Jennifer realized that she was still failing to interest him. She could tell Mary loved the color and design and, she felt, also the deeply religious nature of most of the early paintings exhibited there. "What you see in this gallery," she told them, "marks a revolution in the history of art. Afterward, painting was never the same."

"Yeah, yeah," Herbert muttered, slumped on a bench to one side. "But what difference does it make, huh? They're just dumb pictures."

Jennifer was about to make a calm, reasonable reply when she noticed an unmistakable figure across the gallery, studying a Madonna and Child altarpiece. Her heartbeat increased—and her mind clouded.

Herbert brought her back to earth. "I'm *bored,* Mrs. Denning," he complained in an unpleasant voice. "I don't want to look at this stuff anymore."

Jennifer felt at a loss. Then she remembered Stephen's rapport with Mary that first day. With the two children following in her wake—Mary obediently, Herbert straggling along—she went over to Stephen. "Good morning, Mr. DiRenzo," she said brightly. "Brushing up on medieval art?"

He turned to her with surprise, his expression warm and open. He seemed genuinely pleased to see them. "Yes, as a matter of fact," he replied pleasantly. "I find it refreshing to return to the beginnings, to the simplicity of the Middle Ages."

Herbert, shuffling his feet, surveyed Stephen with suspicion. Neither his look nor his fidgeting were lost on the architect.

"I think that one of your students doesn't agree."

Jennifer responded to the twinkle in Stephen's eyes. "I don't believe you've met Herbert yet," she said calmly, ignoring the boy's impatience. "Mr. DiRenzo is the architect in charge of building the new classrooms at the school," she explained.

Mary smiled at seeing Stephen again, and shook his offered hand shyly. Herbert, true to form, growled, "If you're a real architect, how come you're wasting your time with this art junk, huh?"

"'Art junk,' hmmm?" Stephen echoed thoughtfully. "I have an idea—Herbert, was it?" He looked up at Jennifer questioningly, and she nodded. She didn't quite know what he had in mind, but she was more than willing to see what he could accomplish with Herbert. Winking back at her to seal their complicity, he led the two children toward an exit, saying, "Let's all go out into the piazza, have a soda, and talk about this 'art junk,' okay?"

As the four of them settled down around the table at the nearest café, Stephen continued. "What you don't realize yet, Herbert, is the connection between what you call 'junk' and the real world. Art *is* real, and it's important in our lives."

"Sure, sure," Herbert muttered, unconvinced, blowing through his straw into his soft drink. "Pictures don't have nothing to do with nothing!"

Stephen began unwrapping a package he had with him; the paper was from a bookstore just across the square. "Wrong," he said firmly. "What does that look like to you?" He opened the large book to a page crowded with spidery sepia drawings, then passed it to Herbert. "Anything familiar?"

"Well, sure," the boy said with some enthusiasm. "But this doesn't have anything to do with that art stuff. These look like plans for building some sort of airplane. Or maybe it's a helicopter. Hey! Over here!" He grew more excited. "There are plans for a tank, I think. And these are drawings of guns. Now, this is *neat!*"

Stephen smiled. "It sure is, Herbert. And when do you think these plans were made?"

As the boy paused to ponder the question, Jennifer admired Stephen's approach. Herbert's eyes sparkled with interest.

"Oh, about 1900?" he ventured.

"Nope." Stephen shook his head. "More than four hundred years before the Wright brothers even took off." Herbert whistled. "Do you have any idea who did them?" Stephen asked. The boy shook his head. "Leonardo da Vinci, an artist—and one of the great geniuses of the Renaissance. But he was also a very practical man, in his way. He was an engineer and an architect. Would you like to see some of his architectural drawings?"

"Okay. I really like buildings, you know. But not crummy old buildings so much. I like new buildings. Skyscrapers are really neat."

"Leonardo liked new things, too, Herbert," Stephen replied, his devastating eyes crinkled at the corners. Jennifer felt a sudden urge to reach out and touch his arm—a desire she held in check. "And though he did more work on cathedrals and monuments than he did on skyscrapers, I bet if he'd wanted to build one, he'd have invented the elevator, just to make it possible." Jennifer joined in the general laughter, delighted that Stephen had found a key to opening up this difficult boy.

As they walked back to the spot where Jennifer had parked the VW bus, Herbert asked Stephen almost shyly whether he could borrow the book sometime. "I really like those diagrams," he admitted.

"Sure," Stephen said. "And how would you like to see the kinds of plans *I* work with? If you're interested, I can dig out my original notes for the olive-grove project, *and* the renderings—both the initial sketches and the final ones—and the blueprints. I could show you the whole progression—including the finished buildings. Eventually."

"I'd *like* that," the boy said, showing more positive feeling than Jennifer had seen him display before. "It might even be worth hanging around this dump all summer," he concluded.

Jennifer shook her head, smiling, as the kids piled into the bus. Standing off to one side, she turned to Stephen. "I can't tell you how happy and excited I am that you managed to reach Herbert," she said sincerely. "Frankly, I was beginning to give up hope." She held out her hand. "I don't know how to thank you . . . Stephen."

As he took her hand in both of his, she felt a rush of warmth course through her body. His eyes were an unbelievably pure azure blue, and they seemed to read her thoughts. Her knees felt weak, and she wondered, breathless, whether she would have the strength to withdraw her hand if he didn't release it. "For a start, you could have dinner with me tonight," he replied.

Her first instinct was to refuse, and a biting remark almost escaped her lips. She was suddenly wary of his words at the pool when Mary had first arrived, wary of his behavior today, generous though his efforts with Herbert had seemed. As ridiculous as her suspicions might be, she knew she had reason to be cautious. Her past made her so. But, for heaven's sake, he wasn't asking her to run off with him, only to have dinner. She smiled and met his ice-blue gaze. "That would be lovely. I'd like it very much."

"I'll pick you up at eight," he answered, then turned

and strode away across the piazza. As she watched his strong form get swallowed up by the crowd, she couldn't help wondering whether she'd made the right decision. She hated to admit it, but she already felt a tinge of anticipation.

Jennifer's excitement soared even higher as she and Stephen walked down a breathtakingly beautiful street in the center of Florence. His bare arm grazed hers as they moved side by side, and a warm thrill shot through her.

Stop this nonsense, she warned herself. Despite her awareness of the need to be cautious, she knew she was letting too much ride on this evening. Why couldn't she just relax and enjoy herself? The answer came to her immediately. Jeff.

But all thoughts of her ex-husband fled her mind as soon as she caught a glimpse of the restaurant. It was definitely *not* a tourist spot. No, you had to know that this place was here to find it, hidden away as it was. They entered, and Jennifer looked around appreciatively. The room was small, but the appointments were elegant, the linen snowy, and the waiters impressively deferential. *"Buona sera,* Signor Di-Renzo," the captain said with sincere warmth. "What a pleasure to see you again. I have saved the table you requested."

"Grazie, Aldo," Stephen replied smoothly, placing a firm hand on the small of Jennifer's back that sent shivers down her spine. As they were seated at a corner table, he turned to her and explained easily, "This is one of my very favorite spots. The food is spectacular, because Mamma—Aldo's Mamma, that

is—does all the cooking herself. In fact, she's taught me everything I know about Italian cooking."

As the waiter unfolded Jennifer's napkin and placed it gently on her lap, she reflected that Stephen was obviously known—and genuinely liked—here. She also marveled at how relaxed, how comfortable she felt. Until now, elegant surroundings brought to mind the difficulties she'd had with Jeff's demanding family—and her own very tenuous financial state. But tonight she felt she could enjoy herself. She adopted a teasing tone of voice. "Now, wait just a minute! Don't tell me in addition to being a linguist, an architect, a ballroom dancer, and an amateur teacher, you also cook! I couldn't believe such an assortment of accomplishments!"

He gave her a long, intense look. "And you've just barely scratched the surface," he murmured, then turned to the waiter. *"Chianti Antinori, per favore. Classico,"* he said. To Jennifer, he added, "Of course I cook! How could I survive as a bachelor this long unless I cooked?"

"Some men hire cooks," she suggested thoughtfully, "or eat out or have dozens of willing girl-friends." She smiled impishly into his blue eyes.

"So I've heard," he said noncommittally. "But *I* cook."

She continued to gaze at him, wondering what other hidden talents he possessed—and why he wasn't married.

"And now," he announced, "the story of my life." Jennifer jumped. He really *could* read her mind, she decided. "Sorry," he added with some amusement, taking a sip from his wine glass and nodding at the waiter. "I didn't think that the prospect of my life story would be so startling."

"It's . . . it's . . . just that I was speculating about exactly that," she stammered, "and when you said it, it seemed like ESP or something." She took a sip of her wine, expecting the sharp, acidic bite of Chianti, a taste she had not yet acquired. Instead, the wine was smooth and mellow. "Mmmm, this is delicious," she said in surprise.

"Yes. It's not at all like the cheap stuff you often get. This is vintage Chianti, and it's made from grapes grown right near the villa. Did you know that the Villa Antinori is practically next door? Anyway, about ESP." He lowered his voice and changed the instructive tone to a much more intimate one. "Surely you've noticed that we're on exactly the same wavelength, Jen. I think we're attuned to each other . . . completely. Don't you agree?"

"Well . . . I agree that you've hit on a highly unique approach, Stephen. Or do they still call it 'a line'? Anyway, tell me the story of your life. I really *am* interested in that."

"Okay." He cleared his throat, and she noticed a definite twinkle in his eyes. "My name is Stephen Allen DiRenzo," he began, "and I am thirty-two years old. Born in New York, I became the suave, international sophisticate now before you by having spent my youth in glamorous places—London, Paris, Bologna, and Mexico City, not to mention the time I've put in on the ultra-chic Alaskan frontier. My father was a biologist who took teaching appointments primarily, I think, in order to see the world."

"Oh, I see," Jennifer interjected lightly. "Your

magnificent teaching ability isn't pure accident, then. You've inherited it."

To her surprise, his laughing eyes turned suddenly serious. "I think that when you love something— really love it, whether it's a person or a profession or whatever—then you want to share it with others. Don't you agree? Maybe Herbert will become the next Frank Lloyd Wright. Who knows?" His serious mood passed as quickly as it had come, his pale eyes lightening immediately with laughter. Jennifer was struck once more by what a craggy, good-looking man he was. Jeff was . . . almost pretty, actually, now that she thought about it. But Stephen had the weathered, virile look of an outdoorsman. She remembered how strong his arms had been as he held her on the terrace, and she felt a warm glow starting in the pit of her stomach. She had to know more about him—much, much more.

"Do you have any brothers or sisters?" she asked.

"Two sisters," he replied. "Both older, both married."

"So," Jennifer teased, "you were spoiled by women all your life." She took another sip of wine. She was feeling awfully light-headed, though she knew it wasn't due solely to the Chianti.

"Not at all!" he said, mock hurt in his voice. "In fact, the very reverse is true. Growing up in a household of women has made me especially sensitive to their needs and desires. I've been told that many times!"

Both of them laughed, and Jennifer felt his knee touch hers. The laughter stopped abruptly. "Look at me," Stephen said softly, urgently. He placed a rugged but surprisingly gentle hand on her bare forearm, and her skin tingled pleasurably at his touch. "Now it's your turn," he continued, slowly moving his hand up and down her arm, his eyes, his words, his velvet touch mesmerizing her. Butterflies danced in her stomach and she despaired of ever finding her voice. The rapid change in the tone of their conversation brought a tinge of fear—but also desire.

A sudden motion by Stephen's side broke the spell. Aldo placed a small black telephone on their table. *"Scusi,* Signor DiRenzo," he said. "The call is from Monte Carlo."

Stephen's face changed from its soft melting look into an impassive mask. "DiRenzo here," he barked into the mouthpiece. Jennifer held her breath as he listened for a moment, then he spoke in rapid English. "Don't worry, Vanessa. Certainly I'll be there. I'm leaving right now."

Jennifer's heart sank as a swirl of confused thoughts danced in her head. Leaving? *Now?* And for Monte Carlo at Vanessa's request? Just what kind of hold did she have on Stephen?

As he replaced the receiver and looked up at her, Jennifer could have sworn that, for an instant, he'd forgotten she was there. "Look," he said, "I'm terribly, terribly sorry that a lovely evening has to be spoiled." He smiled, but somehow Jennifer didn't feel his heart was in it. "But I have to catch a plane to-night."

Ever the gentleman—even when he was running out on a lady, she noted wryly—he helped her out of her chair and across the restaurant. After a quick word from him to Aldo, who mortified Jennifer by emitting a cluck of regret as he cast a look of pity in her direction, they were out the door.

Even the cool night air of Florence couldn't lighten Jennifer's burning cheeks. All she wanted was to be safely back in her room at the villa.

They drove silently, Jennifer too stunned to speak, Stephen seemingly already preoccupied by what lay ahead. Though questions about him and Vanessa ran rampant through her mind, Jennifer would be damned if she'd ask him what was going on—especially since he didn't seem to feel any need to fill her in. Finally they pulled into the gracious drive and stopped before the entrance. Jennifer leaped out, unable to bear the thought of Stephen getting out of his seat and rushing over to open the car door for her.

But before she took more than three steps, he reached her. When she didn't stop, he seized her by the shoulders and spun her around to look at him. She cried out at the feel of his hands tight on her flesh, but she refused to look him in the eye. She would never let him know just how much this hurt her, how much she'd wanted this evening to go well.

"Look at me, damn it!" he said, giving her a shake. Mustering all her resolve, she did.

"I've told you I'm sorry and that this is something I can't avoid. I don't know if you believe me or not, but I hope you do." The ice-blue eyes were angry now, and Jennifer took a half-step back. She gasped as he pulled her toward him roughly. "I'll be back as soon as I can, and then we'll get together—I promise." Though his tone made the words more of a threat than an invitation, a thrill of excitement ran through Jennifer. They way he spoke gave her more than a hint of the passion that lay just below Stephen Di-Renzo's usually calm, sophisticated surface.

He moved one hand up behind her head and crushed his mouth to hers. She reeled under the strength of his masculine desire. But before she could respond fully, he had pulled away. The car engine revved up and in a moment she stood in the driveway alone, trembling from his touch—and from her aching, unfulfilled longing for him.

chapter 6

AT LEAST JENNIFER had been wrong about one thing last week when Stephen had left her at the villa. No one had seen her enter the front door and climb the stairs to her room. Thank God for small favors, she thought now as she sat quietly eating lunch with her colleagues. Her silence wasn't, however, entirely self-imposed. Neither she, Don, nor the Hastings could get a word in edgewise in the face of an onslaught of words coming from Vanessa.

"I really can't wait," the brunette was saying. "I haven't seen the count for positively ages." Jennifer caught Don's eyes and she knew he was trying as hard as she was not to laugh. Vanessa had been speaking of her upcoming reunion with her mysterious count to the exclusion of all else, and Jennifer was glad, in a way. That meant Vanessa's connection with Stephen DiRenzo wasn't as strong as Jennifer had feared. But she still didn't know why he had rushed off to Monte Carlo to be with her.

Sam finally managed to cut into Vanessa's monologue by turning to Jennifer and saying, "Well, Jen, we know Vanessa won't be here this evening, and Don's off to that science lecture in Florence, so how would you like to join Marge and me for an elegant dinner in Florence?"

"Thanks for the invitation," Jennifer answered, "but I'd like to just relax tonight. With this heat, I'll probably stay poolside."

"Good idea," Sam said. "I'll arrange for the gardener to set the timer so the pool lights come on as it gets dark."

The diners rose, about to return to the afternoon teaching tasks, when Maria entered. "Signora Denning," she said in her soft voice, "telephone for you."

Jennifer wondered who in the world could be trying to reach her. For an instant she dared to think it might be Stephen, then told herself she was being silly.

"Hello," she said clearly into the receiver. In case the person on the other end of the line was Italian, she wanted to be sure she was understood. She was greeted with a deep, rich rumble of laughter. "Hello," she repeated, unable to keep a hint of impatience from her tone.

"Hi, Jen," a familiar voice said. "This is Steve."

Steve, she repeated to herself. Her pulse raced— with anger as well as excitement. Maybe he was sorry for what had happened last week and was trying to make up for it with a lack of formality, but somehow Jennifer felt that his outburst of laughter was pushing the limits of familiarity.

Before she could respond, he continued. "You'll have to forgive my laughter," he said, and she could just picture the way his blue eyes must be twinkling with amusement. "It's just that you sounded so . . . professional."

She forced herself to remain calm. Why was her pulse racing so fast? "I'm sorry I don't sound the way you'd like me to, Stephen."

If she'd hoped to bait him with those words, she was wrong. He merely laughed again. "I know you have a will of your own," he said. "I was just wondering if I could make amends for my behavior last week—and for a missed meal—by inviting you to my place for dinner tonight."

Like the first time, Jennifer was tempted to refuse. They would be utterly alone in his home, and she was fully aware of where the evening might lead. Yet the desire to see him again won out over her fear of facing his demands. "I'd like that," she said. "If you don't think the heat will be a problem."

"The heat . . ." he echoed, and she could have kicked herself for the unintentional innuendo. "Oh, you mean the weather . . . no, I honestly don't think that'll be too much of a problem." Again he laughed. "Why don't I pick you up at nine?"

Jennifer agreed to the time and hung up. That afternoon, despite her efforts not to think about the evening ahead, she often found herself preoccupied by it. She'd never thought she'd welcome Herbert's loud voice, but she was grateful when his insistent demands forced her attention back to her students.

That evening she chose a soft, scoop-necked pink T-shirt and combined it with a black, flowered cotton skirt that reached just below her knees. Blue shadow highlighted her eyes, and she used just a dab of a dusty-pink-rose blusher on her cheeks.

It was already dark when she spotted Stephen coming across the terrace toward her, and she was glad she'd been sparing in her use of the blush. Her fair skin was burning as she walked over to meet him. Just seeing him made her pulse race and sent tingles of anticipation across her skin. As his warm, strong hands closed over her own and he gazed down at her with his intense blue eyes, the impact of his presence sent her senses reeling. She couldn't believe the effect he had on her. No man had come close to making her feel so alive, so . . . desirable. It was like a gift from heaven. At once she knew without a doubt what he would ask of her that night. And she knew with equal certainty that she would give herself to him. She didn't *want* to resist him. She wanted to forget the past and revel in the present, to put behind her every painful memory and live life with a vengeance.

"Hello," Stephen said quietly, a slow, broad smile spreading over his handsome face. He bent to give her a swift kiss on her still-flushed cheek.

"Hello," she whispered, suddenly shy.

"Are you hungry?" She nodded. "Then come on, let's go." His voice rose with excitement on the last words, and suddenly Jennifer found herself being taken firmly by the hand and racing across the Tuscan countryside. As they rushed along, she inhaled deeply, savoring the sweet smells of dewy grass and the pungent scents of the olive groves and the fruit trees, heavy with apples, peaches, and pears.

"Stephen!" she cried, gasping with delight and excitement. "Slow down! I'm going to break a leg if you keep tearing along like this." He only laughed and swooped her up in his arms to lift her over a fence. He followed in a bound, lost his balance, and pulled Jennifer down with him. She found herself rolling over and over in the new-mown hay, stopping finally on her back, Stephen lying next to her. As their breathing slowed, they gazed up at the ink-dark sky studded with an infinite number of sparkling stars.

"Stephen, look!" Jennifer whispered, pointing. "There's a shooting star!"

"Of course," he replied softly in her ear. "There are always a few of them in the summer months. And they're magical, aren't they? Like our own private fireworks." He raised himself on an elbow, gently brushing strands of golden hair from her cheeks, then slowly brought his mouth down to hers and kissed her deeply.

"Oh, Stephen," she breathed as he moved away to stand up, pulling her up beside him. Without speaking they walked the remaining distance to a small stone structure with a thatched roof. Stephen opened the door, and, though her breath was still coming in short pants, Jennifer made an effort to recover her senses.

"This was the gatekeeper's house," he explained, ushering her inside.

Jennifer glanced eagerly around the large room. The floorboards were extremely wide and pegged, probably very old. The walls were plaster over stone, rough and appealing. Some of Stephen's blueprints hung there, providing the only artistic touch. The room was very neat, she noticed, and a large double bed, covered with a charming peasant-weave blanket, occupied a good deal of the floor space. Huge pillows covered in the same fabric were strewn about as well.

Along one wall ran a row of modern kitchen appliances and counters. A heavy, old armoire and small table and chairs were the only conventional pieces of furniture.

"This is beautiful, Stephen," Jennifer exclaimed. "It's so simple and homey." She stopped, feeling a bit embarrassed as her eyes fell again on the bed.

"Thank you," Stephen answered quietly, as if knowing what she was thinking. "I'm very comfortable here—and I hope you will be, too."

She looked up swiftly to catch his expression, but he turned away and asked lightly, "Now, what would you like to drink?"

She noticed that he was pouring himself some Scotch. "Gin and tonic," she replied quickly. Usually she would have preferred wine, but tonight she felt in need of something stronger.

Stephen handed her the glass and, as their fingers touched, he held her gaze. Then, with a flourish, he directed her to the rustic table which was already set for dinner. He pulled out a chair for her, then moved across to the kitchen. As Jennifer watched him prepare their first course, she was again taken with his lithe body, his economy of movement. In what seemed like no time at all, he was back at the table.

"Madame, dinner is served," he announced as he placed a plateful of fried zucchini on a straw trivet between their two placemats, then sat down opposite her. The zucchini was crisp, light, and delicate, and they ate it with their fingers.

"This is marvelous," Jennifer said. "I'm sure you'll make some woman a fine husband one day."

"Oh, really?" He raised a mocking eyebrow.

"Although with your lifestyle," she continued, "you might have one wife in the United States and others in various cities around the world."

To her surprise, his eyes clouded over at her words, and she noticed a certain tensing of his expression and body. Immediately she regretted her half-teasing, half-serious words, although she didn't understand why they had upset him.

"Sounds tempting," he said sarcastically, his tone guarded. "No, I have no wives, secret or otherwise." Then, to Jennifer's relief, his eyes took on a devilish glint that overpowered his look of cynicism. "But then, I haven't been exactly celibate for all of my thirty-two years," he admitted.

"So I've suspected." Despite her efforts to keep her tone light, it sounded curt even to her own ears. The thought of Stephen with another woman had brought a sharp pain to her heart.

"Do I detect a note of disapproval?" Stephen asked. "What's the matter, Jen? Don't you ever play around?"

"Unlike *some* people, Signor DiRenzo," she replied with some indignation, "I *don't* 'play around.'"

"Not even in...Rome?" he asked, his blue eyes widening in an innocent look.

"You're lucky I'm polite and don't believe in kicking people under the table," she told him at this reference to their first conversation.

"Oh?" he asked. "That's right. If I remember correctly, your specialty is the well-aimed, and, might I add, shapely, heel to the instep. Or am I thinking of somebody else?"

"*Touché!*" she said with a laugh. "But you must admit you deserved that one!"

"I admit to nothing," he countered. "Except, perhaps, that the next course should be ready by now."

"You're a typical male," she replied with a laugh. "When things heat up, you escape to the kitchen!"

He smiled and excused himself from the table. While his back was turned, Jennifer breathed a sigh of relief. She was enjoying their light sparring, but the ever-present tension between them was beginning to wear down her defenses. She wondered briefly once again why her comment about his having many wives had upset him. Did he, perhaps, have his own painful past that he preferred to keep a secret?

When he returned with the next dish, she forced these thoughts to the back of her mind. He was too good at picking up on what she was thinking, which she attributed to the fact that she was cursed with a very readable face. She knew her face lit up with surprise when she saw the pasta course—linguini with what appeared to be a *frutte di mare* sauce. When she tasted it, she was further amazed. The shrimps, scallops, and other seafood, perfectly cooked and bursting with fresh, briny flavor, were bathed in a light tomato sauce spiked with chili and garlic. Stephen followed this dish with a simple breast of chicken *al limone,* its smooth texture and refreshingly tart lemon accent providing a perfect foil to the other dishes.

Jennifer shook her head. "I have to hand it to you, Stephen," she said. "I had no idea you were capable of all this..." She caught his eye and added hastily, "Not that I ever doubted what you said about your cooking."

"Come, come," he said in a mock-scolding tone. "Don't tell me that the signora is a sexist at heart? Is this the sort of person we have teaching our children?"

"Now, hold on a minute, Stephen," she replied, surprised at her defensiveness. "I don't know many people, men *or* women, who can get together a meal like this."

"You're quite right," he interjected. "I'm one of a kind." He placed a hand on her shoulder as she rose to help him clear off the table for their coffee and leaned over to whisper in her ear, "And I don't want you to forget that."

Without thinking, she turned toward him just as his arm slipped around her waist. She wrapped her own arms around his neck and felt her body mold to his. They kissed deeply, his tongue exploring the warm, moist inside of her mouth. Her legs felt weak, and when they broke apart, gasping, she felt as if she might fall, but he kept a strong arm around her. His ice-blue eyes met hers, and he raised his eyebrows in a knowing look. Despite her years with Jeff, she felt inexperienced before Stephen, and, although she craved to learn all he could teach her, she was suddenly desperately afraid of being inadequate. She had never experienced sensations like these before—fires deep inside that threatened to burn out of control and consume every part of her. They frightened her.

Still without speaking, Stephen finished removing the dishes, seemingly heedless of the need he had aroused in Jennifer. He moved about in silence as she sought to control her rapid breathing. Surely he could hear the pounding of her heart! She wanted him so badly, and for a moment she knew he had wanted her, too. But now he didn't seem to be affected by her at all. The tension was unbearable!

Stephen returned to the table with two cups of espresso, glasses, and a bottle of anisette, one plate of coffee beans and another of lemon peels.

"Mosca?" Jennifer asked, trying to sound as natural as possible. She picked up a coffee bean and tossed it in her liqueur glass, continuing to speak, knowing her words came too fast. "I've never understood this tradition," she said. "And to call the beans 'flies' is especially unappetizing. But when in Florence—"

Her words were cut off as he reached across the table in a motion so fast that it startled her. His hand was on her arm, the tightness of his grasp compelling her to look at him. "Don't do this, Jennifer," he said, and she quailed at the intensity of his expression. "Don't act as if nothing has happened. Why do you keep running from the feeling we have for each other? Just what happened between you and your ex-husband—or whoever it was—to make you so frightened?"

She was at a complete loss for words. His sudden change in mood had completely unbalanced her, and she felt threatened and vulnerable before his burning gaze.

Finally Stephen eased the pressure of his hand on her arm. "I'm sorry," he said softly. "I didn't mean to frighten you. But I'd really like to hear the 'story of your life,' as you put it the other night."

His obvious concern, and the fact that he had moved away from her, helped her to relax. She began to feel more in control.

"I have an idea," he said suddenly, his mood changing swiftly once again. He stood up and clasped her hand, pulling her toward the door. "I want to show you something."

Jennifer's curiosity was piqued, but she began to get an idea of where they were going as Stephen helped her into the car and they sped down the hillside into Florence. The wind whipped past Jennifer's face, and she welcomed the coolness against her hot cheeks. Stephen handled the car expertly, heading up a winding road on the opposite side of Florence from Bellosguardo. "Ah," she said, "you're headed for Fiesole."

"And I thought I might surprise you with a new view of the city you love so much," he replied, sounding disappointed.

"It would be hard to have visited Florence before and not have enjoyed this vista," she replied laughing. "That was a long time ago though."

"All right," he said, sounding slightly mollified. Fiesole was considerably higher than Bellosguardo, making the view of Florence even more impressive.

Stephen finally pulled off the road, and they got out of the car. "Just think," he suggested, gesturing grandly as though he were personally responsible for the view, "if you'd never seen this before, you might faint dead away—and that's not at all what I have in mind!"

Jennifer drew in her breath. It didn't matter that she'd been there before. This city looked like a magical fairyland beneath their feet. Streetlights twinkled, and the illuminations of the Duomo, the Pitti Palace, and other monuments glowed warmly. The evening mists made the Arno look like an enchanted river as it wound its way through the center of the city.

Jennifer sank down on an ancient stone wall. "It makes me feel very lucky," she mused, "and also very insignificant."

Stephen moved beside her. "In what way?"

"Lucky to be here, seeing it, taking it all in—but insignificant because it's been here for centuries, unchanged, and will still look just like this long after we're gone."

Stephen seemed to consider her words for a long moment before putting an arm around her shoulder. She felt safe, under his protection. A sensation of warmth moved through her in that increasingly familiar and intoxicating, but also disturbing, way. He pulled her to her feet slowly and turned her toward him. She shivered. "I don't think you're insignificant at all," he said. "In fact, with that beautiful, honest, trusting face, I think you're the most significant thing in this landscape, and I want very much to kiss you and make that troubled look disappear from your eyes." His hands moved up to her face as he leaned down and kissed her, softly at first, but with mounting intensity. Jennifer felt as if all the lights of Florence were exploding in her head. She was melting in the deliciousness of his touch.

Stephen moved away gently, then drew her head against his shoulder. "Jennifer, lovely Jennifer," he whispered, his warm breath caressing her cheek. "You asked for my story the other night. Don't you think it's time you told me about yourself?" He drew back a little and cupped her face with his hands. "Do you trust me enough to share it with me?"

Meeting his steady gaze, Jennifer *did* trust him. Suddenly she wanted to tell him everything. The words spilled out, slowly at first but with increasing ease.

"I'm afraid it sounds a little like a soap opera," she said softly, stepping away from him and staring out across Florence. A burden seemed to lift from her shoulders. It seemed very important that he understand her.

"I grew up in Hartford, Connecticut," she began again. "My father worked in an insurance company on and off. His health was never really very good. He passed away when I was eight, and my mother died just a year and a half later." The pain of these memories made it impossible to look at Stephen. He put his hand on her arm, gently, tenderly caressing her.

"I moved in with my mother's unmarried sister. She was really all the family I had, since my father had been an only child, and I never knew any of my grandparents. In high school I got a waitressing job at the country club. The Dennings belonged to that club—they and their son, Jeff, who was a few years older than I. I guess I wasn't aware of the differences between us at the time. After all, Jeff went to the local high school and was the captain of the tennis team. After work I would play on the club courts, and he took an interest in me. It was such a thrill."

She looked up and into Stephen's eyes. "But once he graduated and went off to Columbia in New York City, I thought that was that. Then I got a scholarship to Barnard—where I met Sam and Marge—and Jeff and I started seeing each other again. By my sophomore year, Jeff was in medical school, and by my junior year we were married.

"We had a horrible little apartment up in Morningside Heights, and he was in class all the time. I got a master's degree, doing secretarial work part-time in various academic offices to help pay the bills. Sam Hastings always saw to it I got first crack at the decent jobs." She paused for breath, uncomfortably aware of Stephen's penetrating gaze. "And I loved my courses and my husband and keeping house and everything. I was really looking forward to teaching, but Jeff insisted that we make it on our own, on *my* salary. We just couldn't afford to have me teach. So I became a fancy 'executive assistant' at an advertising agency on Madison Avenue, and they paid me a very fancy salary to be a good secretary. All the other women hated taking letters and making coffee, but I didn't mind at all. It was easy work, it took my mind off other things, and they loved me because I didn't complain. Pretty soon I was *the* senior secretary in the office, and Jeff and I moved into a larger apartment—and still had money to spare. He graduated, got a good internship, and I was finally able to do some teaching."

Jennifer took another deep breath. "Just when I felt my life was going well, Jeff announced he was in love with a woman doctor he'd gone to school with. Apparently they'd been having an affair for some time. And so I took an unexpected winter vacation and went to the Dominican Republic and got a divorce. And then Sam and Marge and the Hastings School came along, and things began looking up again."

She forced herself to smile and look up at Stephen.

"Your marriage ended just last year?" Stephen asked softly. She nodded. "What a terrible thing to go through. I'm sorry it happened to you. I think there's a special place in hell for unfaithful people," he added harshly.

She was surprised by the deep feeling in his voice. Maybe he really did care, she thought. Or else he felt sorry for her. "As they say in my business," she commented quietly, "it was a learning experience." She tried to smile, but the tears started to fill her eyes.

"Hey, there," he whispered softly, running his hand up and down her back in a soothing caress. She turned toward him and found herself in his arms. What she'd just told him about her marriage was more than she'd ever told anyone, and she felt an incredible sense of relief. Suddenly all the passion she felt for him, all the feelings she'd tried to deny for so long, broke free.

She lifted her mouth to his and their lips met in a sweet kiss that became hungry, demanding. He moved his head away from hers for a moment, and she saw that his blue eyes had none of their usual mocking look, but instead were deep pools of tenderness. "Oh, Stephen..." she moaned, and melted into his embrace, the memory of her life with Jeff becoming more and more faint with each stroke of his healing hands.

"You've been through a lot lately," he whispered. "But I hope you haven't built too thick a wall around yourself. Not everyone is cruel and unfaithful, you know." His slender, strong fingers continued to stroke the back of her neck and her shoulders, underneath the silky knot of her hair, and she was melting, throbbing, glowing at his touch. "Let's go back," he whispered huskily. She followed him silently to the car.

Once she looked over to find Stephen giving her a half-commanding, half-entreating look, as if he wasn't sure she would actually give herself to him when they returned. She smiled tremulously and squeezed his hand, already feeling the insistent throb of desire. How she anticipated the thrill of being with him, of making love. She felt her cheeks go scarlet, but her eagerness didn't fade.

At last Stephen parked in front of the cottage, and they walked inside, hand in hand. As the door closed behind them, shutting them together in the dimly lit room, Stephen reached for her, pulling her gently but firmly against his body. "Oh, Jen, how I've wanted this, wanted you . . ."

He released the pin holding up her hair and it tumbled down around her shoulders in a golden cascade. He grasped the luxuriant fall and kissed her fiercely, demanding both her body and her soul in his searing embrace. His hands moved down her back, then up again underneath the T-shirt. His touch felt like fire on her swollen breasts and taut nipples, and she moaned softly, clinging to him. He moved his mouth to her ear and ran his tongue around the rim until she gasped, feeling the reverberations in the pit of her stomach and below.

Now his hands were at her waist, where he unhooked her skirt deftly. As it fell to the floor, he slipped the T-shirt over her head, pausing to gaze at her standing naked except for her bikini panties. *"Che bella,"* he said. "Like one of Raphael's saints." He picked her up and lowered her to the bed, then took off his own clothes, his eyes never leaving her. Her flushed skin deepened in color when he stood before her, tall and magnificent and ready for her.

Finally he lit a candle and stretched out next to her, close but not touching. "I want to see you," he murmured, tracing a path with his finger from her mouth, down over her chin, through the hollow of her throat, between her breasts, across her stomach, and beyond...

As if compelled, she moaned again, the pleasure he was generating with his sensitive fingers overcoming her. "Oh, Stephen," she murmured, "I want you so..." Feeling a terrible sense of urgency, she rolled on top of him, surprised at her audacity. "I need to feel you against me, please." His strong hands against her back pressed them together, and, emboldened by her success, she began kissing his face more and more fiercely, feeling his virile strength and wanting desperately to be taken, to be carried to the heights of passion.

Suddenly he was on top of her, stroking her body into a frenzy of sensation. "Now! I want you *now!*" she almost sobbed, thinking she could stand no more. But the tide continued to rise.

"Don't be too anxious, my love," he breathed. "We have all the time in the world. We have all night. And I plan to use every minute." And then they were riding together, sharing the exquisite sensations as one body, one soul, and the wave broke, again and again and again, causing Jennifer to cry out in ecstasy.

"Oh, Stephen!" she murmured.

"And the next time will be even better," he whispered, "and the next and the next..." He held her tightly in his arms, and she was aware of the wonderful slippery feeling of their skin together. She brushed a damp strand of hair out of his eyes, and he kissed her. "You're so beautiful."

She closed her eyes—just for a moment, she thought—and was awakened from a catnap by the gentle explosion of a cork popping. She sat up, smiling. Stephen was sitting on one of the pillows next to the bed with a bottle of sparkling Italian wine. "And what are we celebrating?" she asked, almost bursting with happiness.

"Why, our fantastic lovemaking, of course," he teased. "Can you think of anything better?" He reached over and kissed her.

"No, nothing," she acknowledged, but privately she wondered if that was all it meant to him—great sex. But she felt so incandescent, as if a huge candle were glowing inside her, that she decided not to think about imaginary problems. She took a sip from the glass he offered her, and the bubbles tickled her nose. She giggled, then leaned happily against Stephen as he began to trace the outline of her nipples. Desire engulfed her in a rush, taking her by surprise. She turned to him, running her hands down the sides of his smooth, hard chest. She felt fierce and powerful.

"Ready for some more, are you?" he said, moving his fingers down to her navel. "Fortunately, we have plenty of time." He moved aside their glasses. "I may not stop all night."

"Good," she sighed, reaching for him once again.

Jennifer awoke just as the light of early day moved across the bed, enticing her eyes open and gilding the dark head next to her on the pillow. She stretched drowsily and shifted slightly, smiling as Stephen altered his position to accommodate her movements, yet stay within her embrace. She watched him sleep, his chiseled features relaxed, one arm arched above her head, the fingers bent, one leg thrown possessively across her hips. She sighed deeply. How she loved him...

Immediately her thoughts sharpened, as if she'd been thrown into icy water. *She loved him!* A tremor shot across her heart as that one word—love—let open a floodgate of dark and painful memories. Once she had loved Jeff, loved him with her body and all her heart, and he had used her and then rejected her. In minutes he had destroyed the very foundations of her existence and thrown into doubt her sense of worth as an individual and as a woman.

And now what had she done? For one brief night, she had put aside the past and lived for the moment, glorying in sensations she hadn't known were possible. For a few short hours she'd known a happiness that burst the bounds of any happy moments that had gone before. And in that short time, the strange, overwhelming attraction she had felt for Stephen DiRenzo had turned into love. As if manipulated by cruel, whimsical gods, the passion she had called a gift from heaven had become twisted into a love that made her vulnerable to rejection, an unguarded target for destruction.

But no, she reasoned, glancing again at Stephen's sleeping form, Jeff and Stephen were different people. Just last night, at Fiesole, Stephen had been angry to learn of Jeff's betrayal and had condemned all unfaithful people to a special place in hell.

But as Jennifer considered further, new doubts crept into her thoughts. From the very beginning, Stephen's intentions had been to seduce her. He hadn't tried to hide the fact, but as she thought about it now, she wondered if the concern he had expressed for her had been sincere—or a clever weapon to add to his arsenal of kisses and caresses, all skillfully employed in a campaign to get her into bed. After all, he had openly admitted to having had many other women before her. And he had never explained the phone call at dinner that had taken him to Vanessa in Monte Carlo. Most important of all, in his impassioned murmurings, he had never said, "I love you"—only "I want you."

All at once, Jennifer knew she had to get away. If he awoke before she left and took her in his arms, she might be lost again. And she must never let that happen. She had made that mistake once. She never would again.

She slid carefully from the bed and moved noiselessly about the room, dressing quickly in the early-dawn light. When she was fully clothed, she stood looking down at Stephen, her shoes in her hand. He appeared so relaxed and vulnerable that she yearned to stay with him, to trust him not to break her heart. But she couldn't—she just couldn't.

As she turned to go, the shoes she was holding knocked against the back of a chair. Her heart leaped into her throat and her eyes darted to the bed.

She stood poised for flight as Stephen turned groggily, felt for where she had lain, and, not finding her, sat up with a start. Then he saw her and a slow smile spread across his face. But gradually it turned to a frown, as if he had sensed the change in her.

"Good morning," he said guardedly. "Why aren't you in bed with me? Where are you going?"

"I'm going back to the villa," she told him simply. "I have classes to teach."

"But what's your hurry? It's early." He sat up in bed, pulling the sheet up around his middle. She flushed at the sight of his naked chest.

"I have to go back, Stephen," she insisted. "Our little fling is over, and now it's time to return to the real world."

"The real world...our little fling," he repeated, his anger rising. "What are you talking about? What's gotten into you since last night? Last night! Hell, it was only a few hours ago." In a swift movement, he was out of bed, holding her firmly by the shoulders. She tried to twist out of his grasp, but he held her still and forced her to meet his angry eyes. "Look at me, Jennifer," he demanded. "I want to know what this is all about."

"It's not about anything," she retorted, breaking free of him at last. "I had a nice time last night, but it's over now. I'm an independent woman making it on my own." She paused uncertainly, then added in a near-whisper, "You cloud my mind considerably."

She had meant this last to soften her previous statements, but he obviously didn't take it that way. "God forbid you should have anything but a clear mind," he replied sarcastically.

"I . . . I just meant that you have a strong effect on me. That when we're together I seem to forget who I am . . ." The hardness of his voice confused her. Why did he have to make this more difficult than it already was?

"Can't you see you have a similar effect on me?" he demanded.

"But it's different for you," she protested, and became appalled when she realized she had almost told him her *real* reason for leaving. "I'm sorry," she finally murmured, falling back on an old defense. "I'm just not ready for a serious involvement. I have other priorities—the children, Marge and Sam, my career. They have to come first." There was a long silence. "I'd better go now."

"I can't quarrel with your commitment to teaching," he said at last in a voice so cold that it cut right through her. "But it's a big mistake to put professional priorities before personal ones." He came closer, and, lifting her chin with one finger, gazed deep into her eyes. She could tell he was still furious. "Perhaps we should just be pen pals," he said with scathing mockery. "You see, I have a long-standing aversion to single-minded career women. I hope you decide that the role doesn't suit you at all. Now go before I lose my temper." He turned her firmly toward the door, and she walked back across the fields toward the villa, blind to the beautiful morning and feeling numb to her very bones.

* * *

Jennifer returned to her room and threw herself across the bed. Several hours later, she woke up still feeling troubled and confused. How could she have become so involved with Stephen DiRenzo in such a short time?

Wearily, she pulled herself out of bed. When she had mentioned her career to him, she had scarcely expected him to turn so mocking and sarcastic. Why had he had such a strong reaction against her commitment to her work? Even thought she had used it to hide her real reason for leaving, her career *was* important to her. Obviously, this was simply another unresolved conflict between them, another reason to stay away from him.

As she brushed her hair vigorously back into a single ponytail, she squared her shoulders with determination. Yet a hollow feeling persisted deep inside, where last night there had been a raging fire. The thought of his touch still made her arms tingle, and the memory of his lips sent a flush across her face. It would be madness to come under his intoxicating spell again!

chapter 7

JENNIFER SMILED WANLY at her reflection in the mirror, noticing that the gray-green blouse and tan skirt she'd put on looked drab and washed out and that she had faint circles under her eyes. So much for the salutary effects of passion, she thought ruefully, disturbed that just thinking about Stephen DiRenzo had the power to call up such strong feelings in her.

Jennifer felt better when she arrived downstairs and saw Don Allison's pleasant, uncomplicated face at the breakfast table. She greeted him warmly. "Hi, Don," she said, choosing a plain roll to have with her steaming *caffè-latte,* the half-coffee, half hot-milk combination she loved. The milk formed a bubbly froth on the surface of the brew, and a slight dusting of cinnamon added a piquant taste.

"It sure feels like summer today," she said with

false brightness, "and the city is going to be an oven, I'm afraid. But I've promised Mary that we'd take a look at some of the *other* churches in Florence—after our obligatory stop at the Duomo, of course." Jennifer smiled, relieved to get her thoughts off her own problems. "I think Mary would move in there if she could. She must feel very safe there. I'll be interested to see if any of the other churches has a similar effect on her."

"She still doesn't talk?" Don asked. Jennifer nodded. "I think you're going to reach her," he continued hopefully. "Soon." He paused. "Listen, Jennifer, you're right about this weather. It's going to be hot and sunny right through the weekend. Would you like to drive to Viareggio with me tomorrow? I haven't seen the coastline, and though I hear it's not quite the Riviera, it *is* a beach."

"What a good idea," Jennifer replied, welcoming the chance to escape the school, Florence—and Stephen. "I'd love to! And it's a fine beach, or at least it was a number of years ago. Of course, I've never been to the Riviera."

"Cannes and Nice are simply horrible," Vanessa offered huskily, just entering the room. "Overcrowded tourist traps with *nothing* to recommend them. But there are still some very nice, elegant little spots along the French coast, if you know where to go. But, then, when one visits the Riviera, one usually does it on a large yacht and avoids the beach problem altogether." She smiled brightly and poured herself black coffee.

"Well, now we know," Don said with a straight

face. "So we'll be doubly appreciative of Viareggio tomorrow."

The day did turn out hot and humid. By the late-afternoon rest period, Jennifer was more than ready for a swim. As she changed into her suit, gratefully throwing her sticky blouse and skirt into the laundry hamper, she hoped that everyone else was taking a nap. She longed to have the pool to herself, to forget the hurt and confusion she felt over Stephen by swimming ten or fifteen fast laps and then floating lazily, staring up at the sky.

As she approached the diving board, she noted with satisfaction that she was alone. Using a modified racing dive, she knifed through the water, reveling in the refreshing shock of the cold water against her hot skin. She began a fast, efficient crawl toward the shallow end, executed a flip turn, and started back, allowing the water to caress her body all over. Idly, she wished that she didn't have to wear a suit, imagining the sensuous luxury of swimming naked.

Gradually her weariness and tension began to leave her body, as they always did when she was able to get some vigorous exercise. She did love the students, but shepherding several of them around a blistering hot Florence for most of that day had been a strain, especially after her nearly sleepless night and continuing emotional turmoil.

The sudden memory of Stephen DiRenzo's arms around her the evening before made her tingle. She told herself firmly to forget him. She couldn't afford to take the chance of loving him. Not after Jeff.

She began her final lap, then flipped over on her back and floated, gazing at the few puffy clouds drifting high above and enjoying the kiss of the warm sun on her upturned face.

Suddenly her quiet moment was shattered. "I spent the morning with Herbert," Stephen said calmly from somewhere behind her, out of view. His unexpected voice startled Jennifer so completely that she folded up at the waist, dunking herself in the process. She came up sputtering, embarrassed and furious. She splashed over to the side and hauled herself up, tight-lipped, refusing to acknowledge that he had upset her equilibrium.

"He still seems really excited by the work," Stephen continued matter-of-factly, "and by the prospect of monitoring the whole construction process."

He was wearing ordinary bathing trunks today, Jennifer noticed, and she couldn't help admiring the long, sleek lines of his slender but well-muscled body, remembering how it had felt pressed against her. "I'm glad the two of you get along," she finally managed in a calm voice, drying her hair with the towel she had brought along. If he could act as if nothing important had happened between them since the day before, so could she. "I appreciate your taking the time with him," she added casually.

Stephen walked lazily over to the diving board, took a high bounce, and sailed gracefully into the air, entering the water with scarcely a ripple. He swam to the other end, returned, and surfaced right beside her. "You swim beautifully," he said. "I was watching you do your laps."

"Didn't anyone ever tell you it's rude to spy on people?" she snapped.

"What's rude," he replied, catching and holding her gaze, "was my behavior this morning. You said something that reminded me of an incident that happened some time ago, and I reacted badly. But I was upset and angry at your leaving me like that. I still don't understand it."

His directness completely nonplused Jennifer and strengthened her fears. She mustn't give in to his charms. But how could she fight him when he was so warm and appealing? Even now she longed to show him just how much she cared for him. She forced a coolness that she did not feel into her voice.

"I guess we aren't so attuned to each other, after all," she said, hedging and determined not to explain what she felt and why she intended to avoid him as much as possible.

"Oh, I think we're very much in tune," he answered, kissing the palm of her hand and sending shivers all the way up her back. "Maybe that's what's scary—to both of us. Whatever the case, I really want to see you again. Let's spend tomorrow together. It's Saturday, and you're off, aren't you?"

"Yes . . . but I'm afraid I've made other plans. I'm going to Viareggio with Don." She was relieved to have an excuse. She mustn't be alone with him!

"Oh," he said shortly. "I am disappointed. I think there's an awful lot for us to talk about . . ."

For a moment Jennifer thought he was going to ask her to break the date, but he kept still. Abruptly, he pulled himself out of the water and stalked over to the wall, where he had dropped his towel.

Jennifer spoke cautiously. "There will be plenty of time for us to get together later. Maybe in a few days we'll have a better perspective on . . . things."

"Oh, I see," he said thoughtfully. "You're calling for a cooling-off period, is that it?" His voice turned harder. "Well, I don't approve of that plan of action. Or inaction, which is really the case." He stepped into his sandals and threw his towel around his neck. "Call it what you like, Jennifer—perspective or breathing space or whatever—but you're running away. From us. One thing you should learn about me is that I never run away from things. I tackle them, head-on. And I never avoid difficulties or . . . challenges." He cocked his head, and his expression was arrogant and determined.

Was that what she was to him? A challenge?

He turned toward the construction site. "I'll let you know if there are any startling developments with Herbert, our budding architect," he called over his shoulder as he strode purposefully away.

Don and Jennifer got an early start the following morning, a day that promised to be hot and cloudless. It was fortunate, Jennifer reflected ruefully, that they were on the road so soon, since Don's aging automobile didn't make very good time, even on the smooth, high-speed *autostrada* that led to the coast. It was a far cry from Stephen's racy sports car, she couldn't help thinking, then instantly felt ashamed of her disloyalty. "Did you buy this car here?" she asked Don politely, trying to get her mind off Stephen.

"I certainly did," Don replied with a laugh. "The

fact is, you can't buy this model outside Italy—new *or* used. Apparently, it doesn't meet United States standards for automobiles or something. But don't worry," he added hastily, catching a glimpse of Jennifer's concerned face. "It's not the strongest machine in the world, but it runs just fine. And I'm a very safe driver."

Jennifer leaned back, reassured. Don was so dependable, he would *have* to be a careful driver. "I'll bet you were president of your class in high school," she guessed.

"Nope." He flashed her a broad grin. "President of the student council. How did you know?"

"You're just so...so...trustworthy." Considering her doubts about Stephen, she doubly appreciated Don's steadfastness. "Why did you choose to go into teaching?"

"First of all, because I really love kids," he replied thoughtfully, "but also because I didn't like the pressure of doing scientific research or of office jobs. I guess I don't have a whole lot of ambition. And since I don't require a lot of money to be happy, and since I would actually *hate* being famous or powerful, I suspect I've found the right spot for myself."

Don's life did seem to suit him, Jennifer reflected. He had a nice, natural way with the children. Of course, given his sunny disposition, she would expect him to be a successful teacher. Not like Stephen, she thought, whom she would never have picked as even a one-time lecturer. But Stephen had the special something—charisma, perhaps—necessary to reach Herbert. And he also had a sensitive side to his nature, one that he hid whenever he thought someone might notice. Then he turned arrogant and mocking instead. Still . . . she had to admit she wished she were in the red Alfa-Romeo with Stephen, speeding . . . somewhere.

"What?" she asked, forcing her attention back to Don, whose last comment she had missed entirely. It was too bad that he couldn't create the kind of excitement in her that Stephen did. He would be so much easier to get along with!

"I said I thought we could stop for lunch before we actually collapse on the beach," Don repeated. "If it's all right with you. Sam told me there's a nice little café quite near the ocean, just north of Viareggio."

"Fine." Jennifer remembered the place. Sam and Marge had taken her there with the kids that summer so long ago. It was a plain wooden building with a spacious, wraparound wooden porch, and the food— especially the seafood—was terrific. As they entered the town, Don drove more slowly.

"Not terribly chic, is it?" he asked, surveying the tired-looking buildings that made up most of downtown Viareggio. "Scarcely Monte Carlo. Not that I know firsthand, you understand," he added hastily. "We'd have to ask Vanessa about that."

"But the beach here *is* very nice," Jennifer reassured him. Don made a right turn and headed out of town. Soon they pulled up by the *ristorante* Sam had suggested and found themselves a pleasant table in the shade, overlooking the beach. The waiter arrived and handed them menus, and Don ordered wine.

"I can barely get by with my two years of college Italian," Don explained unselfconsciously. "And since there's practically no word on this menu that's in my vocabulary, I think you'd better order."

Jennifer glanced down the card quickly. "This place specializes in fresh local seafood," she explained, "and you probably didn't learn the names of a lot of fish in your Italian classes." When the waiter returned, she asked him what was especially fresh that day, then ordered a number of dishes. "We're starting with a *zuppa di pesce*," she began, "which is—"

Don held up his hand. "Don't tell me," he said, savoring the wine. "I want to be surprised."

Laughing and bantering, they enjoyed lunch. Don really *was* good company, Jennifer realized, since he never seemed serious about anything.

Suddenly Don stopped chewing with his mouth full. His face seemed to pale beneath his healthy tan. He swallowed with some difficulty, then pointed to the serving bowl from which he had just helped himself. "Uh...Jennifer...what is it we're eating?" he asked. "I thought it was french fries, but..."

Jennifer burst out laughing. "Aren't they good?" she teased. "They're *calamari*, Don, and if you hadn't seen a whole one there, on the plate, you would never have thought twice about eating baby squid. Admit it! They're delicious!"

"Well, uh..." He gulped. "I'm eating squid? You don't see many squid in the Midwest, Jennifer. And I'm just a country boy at heart. But I will try to broaden my horizons." Bravely, he took another one, closed his eyes, and popped it into his mouth. When he opened his eyes, he was smiling. "See? You can teach an old dog new tricks," he said triumphantly. "They *are* good. Even though I know what they are."

He helped himself to more. "Well, what do you know!" he exclaimed, looking past Jennifer's shoulder. "It's a small world, isn't it? Look who's joining the party!"

Turning in her chair, Jennifer's heart sank. Stephen was helping Vanessa out of the shining Alfa-Romeo. Suddenly the day felt much hotter, and her mouth went unexpectedly dry. She took a quick sip from her wineglass while observing the other couple. As Vanessa stepped onto the gravel parking area, dressed in extremely brief black shorts and a bright red halter top, she leaned heavily on Stephen's proffered arm and gazed raptly into his smiling face. Jennifer couldn't help feeling a stab of jealousy and wondered just how well those two were acquainted.

Don was waving cheerfully, and Stephen steered Vanessa over to their table. Jennifer thought that the small brunette looked less than thrilled with the development, but she sat down when Doug suggested they join them. "I've just been introduced to squid," he announced, "and I am feeling very cosmopolitan. What a pleasant coincidence! You're also planning to enjoy the beach, I presume?"

"That was the general plan," Vanessa replied dryly. "And it's a relief to see that the oceanfront is more inviting than the town back there. I could scarcely believe that the Italians consider *that* a resort!"

"Not all of us have your sophisticated frame of reference, Vanessa," Stephen said teasingly, taking the chair next to Jennifer. His thigh brushed against her leg as he sat down—and he kept his leg next to hers. Just what was the idea, Jennifer thought, furious.

She shifted slightly in her chair, moving her leg away. Stephen shot a mocking glance at her.

"Try to think of this as a pleasant local beach," he continued, addressing Vanessa, "rather than comparing it with Hawaii or someplace, hmmm?" He turned to Don and Jennifer. "Actually, we'll be heading a few miles north, once we've had something to eat." He paused long enough to order some food and another bottle of wine. "Work has just been completed on a house I designed on the coast here, and Vanessa wanted to have a look. So did I, as a matter of fact. Why don't you two come along? The property has its own beach, of course, and it's more comfortable to change in a house than in the back seat of a Fiat, don't you agree?" Jennifer felt impaled by his gaze.

"Jen?" Don asked politely.

"It sounds very nice," she managed to say, intrigued by the idea of seeing a house that Stephen had designed. She was sure that, just like his cottage, it would be special, and she hoped it might tell her more about the sometimes inscrutable man who had created it. It wouldn't hurt to get to know him, she reasoned, as long as they weren't alone together...

"The client is a wealthy Italian businessman," Stephen went on to explain. "And the location presented an interesting challenge." Jennifer was intrigued, but Vanessa just looked bored. Could Stephen really be interested in her, Jennifer wondered. He still hadn't said anything about his mad dash to Monte Carlo, and exactly what Vanessa had to do with it.

Jennifer gazed at Vanessa, who looked extremely cool and chic in her halter and shorts, and wished she herself hadn't worn cut-off blue jeans and a faded T-shirt over her bathing suit. Suspecting Vanessa had brought a practically invisible bikini to wear on the beach, she regretted, too, her own sensible tank suit. She refocused on the group.

Stephen had just drained his wineglass. "Are we ready to go? Just follow us, Don," he ordered, throwing some money down on the table. Don scrambled to do likewise. "I'll be sure and slow down for you!"

"Don't worry," Don replied, "we'll keep up." As the Alfa-Romeo accelerated out of the parking lot, he turned to Jennifer and added in a good-natured voice, "Of course, I may burn out the transmission in the effort..." He laughed and Jennifer was once again struck by his easy-going attitude.

"You know," she noted, "you're a very good sport, Don. About squid and about fast cars..."

"I don't waste my energy getting offended about nothing, if that's what you mean. Besides, Stephen was just kidding me about this old heap. He's mentioned before that he thinks it's an eyesore. And I told him that we solid Midwestern types don't waste our hard-earned money on flashy racing cars. So we're about even. I like DiRenzo, I really do. He's a little prickly sometimes, I guess, and I don't think I'd trust him around my sister, but I enjoy his company. And I think Vanessa's just right for him. I mean, she can handle his... approach, if you know what I mean. She moves in the fast lane, too."

Jennifer's heart twisted with anguish at Don's unknowingly painful comment. Obviously she wasn't the only one who had noticed something going on between Stephen and Vanessa. "I think our Vanessa's more likely to be the thrower than the receiver of a pass," Jennifer retorted to hide her hurt. But to herself she admitted that Don was probably right. Stephen *was* too smooth and sophisticated for her. She couldn't even tell when he was being sincere and when he was teasing.

Don followed Stephen's sports car down a long, winding private lane and came to a halt in a circular driveway that fronted a modest, one-level rectangular box. Massive mahogany doors, burnished so carefully that they seemed to glow, looked almost out of place on the small structure. Then Jennifer noticed that they were on a bluff, perhaps a hundred feet or more above the sea. She heard the surf pounding faintly below, its steady rhythm an almost hypnotic undercurrent.

"Well?" Stephen asked as they joined him at the front doors. "What do you think?"

"It's very . . . simple," Don began, groping for words. Vanessa burst out laughing. Clearly, Jennifer thought, she and Stephen had already discussed the design of the house.

With a flourish, Stephen threw open the doors, and Jennifer gasped. The rectangular structure, she realized, was simply the entrance to a spectacular house that opened up below them. They stood at a balcony that overlooked the magnificent living room. The house was built into the side of a hill descending to the water so that very little of it was visible from the road. A curving, free-standing staircase led down into the main space, a three-story room with a huge fireplace on one rough-brick wall and an open kitchen on the other. The back wall was almost entirely glass, sparkling in the sun and offering a spectacular view of the ocean. Most of the furniture was built in—soft, carpeted platforms and upholstered banquettes arranged in comfortable groupings. A dining table and chairs separated the main area from the kitchen.

"There's another floor beneath this," Stephen explained, "where the bedrooms are. I'd be happy to lead a tour if anyone is interested." He cast a meaningful glance at Jennifer, and she was horrified to feel herself blushing. "After all," he continued to Jennifer as the others walked ahead, "bedrooms are always the most interesting rooms in the house, don't you agree?"

"Depends on who's in them . . . and why," she retorted, moving quickly ahead of him.

It was a wonderful house, Jennifer had to admit after the inspection. The living room was open to the elements, dramatic, and functional yet luxurious, and the private rooms were just that—private—ministering to other human needs. The contrast between the spaces gave the house a special rhythm, she decided as she slipped off her jeans and T-shirt in a cozy apricot-colored bedroom with twin beds and light-colored wooden bureaus. She was about to lift the shade and enjoy the view again when Stephen's voice made her whirl toward the door.

"Do you really like it?" he asked almost shyly. Immediately she felt awkward and vulnerable, standing so near him in her swimsuit. He had changed into a bathing suit, too, and his bare chest, long legs, and the enticing line of hair down his chest took her breath away and sent her pulse racing.

"Oh, yes," she said, her voice hardly more than a whisper. "It's beautiful, Stephen." Suddenly the room seemed too small for both of them, as if the walls were closing in. He closed the door behind him and she felt trapped, like a small, fragile animal being stalked by a panther. Her back was against the window as he started to cross the room toward her. "It must give you enormous satisfaction to see it all completed and furnished and ready to be lived in," she began to babble, finding it difficult to think clearly. Try as she might, she couldn't break loose from his steady blue gaze.

He paused at the end of one bed. "Yes," he said, hypnotizing her with his voice. "It's very satisfying to see it finished." He started moving toward her again. "And to share it . . . with you." As if in a dream, he touched her lips with a long, slender forefinger. Slowly, as if against her will, she melted into his arms. She felt the hardness of his bare chest against her breasts, and her nipples grew taut. He groaned in response. His lips crushed down on hers, and his insistent tongue took possession of her mouth before he pulled back.

"I want you so much," he whispered urgently. "I must have you again. Here. In my house."

She slid her arms up his naked back, pressing the length of her body against him. His hands caressed her back and over her thin swimsuit. She was nearly faint with desire, thinking only of her need to be with him. Abruptly, Vanessa's husky voice, outside in the corridor, broke the spell, and Jennifer came back to reality with a crash, horrified at how she had let herself go and at the thought that Vanessa might have come in on them.

"Where *is* everyone?" Vanessa repeated impatiently. "I, for one, am ready for a swim!"

"What am I thinking of?" Jennifer gasped, pushing

away from him and picking up her towel.

"The same things I am," Stephen replied hoarsely, coming up behind her. "Passion, desire, pleasure..."

"Not here! Not now! We're not alone. What if Vanessa or Don came in? I'd be mortified! Don't you have any sensitivity?" Jennifer strode toward the door, but he got there first.

"I can take care of the crowd," he whispered, "but I'm not sure I can deal with your other objections." He began to sound angry. "As I see it, the facts are simple. We want each other. And the other night showed just how good we can be together..." His eyes became hooded, his tone insinuating.

Jennifer had to force herself to break away from his gaze. "Please leave me alone, Stephen," she said harshly.

"What do you want?" he demanded. "To be buddies? Well, I don't." He turned abruptly and left the room.

Jennifer raised trembling hands to her flushed cheeks and breathed in deeply, trying to slow her galloping heartbeat. She went into the adjoining bathroom and splashed cold water on her face, needing the shock of it against her burning skin, then ran a comb through her hair. *Love*. That was the word he hadn't mentioned. Not once. He was only interested in possession, domination, physical satisfaction. What had he said the day before? He didn't run away, that was it. He faced things head-on. And he was probably used to getting what he wanted. And since he'd had her once, he now assumed she'd be willing whenever he was ready.

Her face in the mirror turned more determined as

she clenched her teeth. She wouldn't be used! She craved the feel of his body against hers, yearned to know again the sweet delight of their time together. She wanted to know him, to love him . . . to have him love her. She felt a tear at the corner of one eye and she brushed it away angrily. Shaking her head, she turned toward the door. Jeff had used her to keep house and pay the bills. She wasn't going to be used again. Not for sex. Not for anything. She hurried to catch up with the others.

Outside, stairs cut into the bluff itself led down to a private beach. "What a marvelous location," Vanessa said, carefully arranging herself on a huge beach towel. Jennifer smiled nervously, noticing the revealing white bikini Vanessa wore.

"The location was one of the main reasons I accepted the commission," Stephen explained patiently, obviously in full control of himself once again, Jennifer noted wryly. "Because I knew it was the perfect site for the house I wanted to build," he went on.

Looking back at the structure from the beach, Jennifer saw how gracefully it nestled into the hillside, its blond-wood and glass exterior echoing the beige of the sand and the glint of the water below. "What were your other reasons?" she asked very softly, wanting to know more about him in spite of herself.

He didn't seem to hear her question. "I'm going for a swim," he growled.

Jeff had been sure of himself, too. Always certain he was right, no matter who got hurt. She closed her eyes against the blinding sun and breathed in the sharp, salty sea air.

Stephen returned from his swim as abruptly as he had left and briskly toweled himself off without speaking a word, his expression stern but no longer glowering.

"I was explaining to Jennifer and Don that Signor Rinaldo let you make all the decisions about the house," Vanessa said brightly. "Oh, since you're up—would you mind?" She held out a bottle of suntan lotion for Stephen to rub on her back. With a grunt of assent, he applied himself to the task, demonstrating, Jennifer thought, a great deal of enthusiasm for the job. His hands looked very large on Vanessa's small back. Large and possessive.

"I can't imagine that most clients are willing to give that kind of *carte blanche*," Vanessa continued, shading her eyes to look up at Stephen. "This must have been a very special case."

"It was, to a certain extent," he admitted, wiping his hands on Vanessa's towel, then stretching out on his own. "But I demand a lot of independence from clients. If they don't like my design, they can get another architect. I don't compromise." He closed his eyes.

"You're used to getting your own way," Jennifer thought idly, and was immediately appalled to realize she'd spoken the words aloud.

Stephen shot a piercing look. "Yes, I am," he said firmly, meaningfully. "And if something is important to me, I won't give up until I do get it. I'm proud of my powers of persuasion."

"Nobody wins *every* battle," Jennifer retorted pointedly, rolling over onto her stomach.

"True. But I win all the important ones." He

sounded very sure of himself. "You just have to know what you want—and how to go after it."

"It's not always that simple," Don interjected. "A lot of us have to think about paying the rent along with getting what we want." Jennifer was relieved to find that the conversation had taken a less personal turn, but this new topic was an uncomfortable one for her as well.

"I've never had to worry about money myself," Vanessa replied lazily. "Since Daddy is in oil, I can't imagine not being able to pay the rent. It must be dreadful. I'd go to great lengths to avoid it, even if it meant making a small compromise here and there."

"Sometimes you can't avoid money problems, even if you make compromise after compromise," Jennifer heard herself say in a small voice. The bitterness of her tone surprised her as much as the confession.

Don came to her rescue. "You've got to realize how fortunate you are, Vanessa," he said quickly, directing their attention back to the tiny brunette. "Most of us have to work for a living and then live on what we earn. Now, some of us spend our extra cash on flashy cars," his voice became teasing, "while others of us squirrel it away for a rainy day. Tell me, why did you go into education? As a hobby?"

Vanessa seemed taken by surprise. "Me?" she asked. "Well, I was always interested in science, of course. I found, though, that I liked the social sciences more than the physical ones, and so I went into psychology. And then I got interested in performance capacities in laboratory animals, and genetic versus learned disabilities. . . ." Her voice trailed off. "Pass me that suntan lotion, will you, Stephen?"

Jennifer sat up and stretched. She refused to watch Vanessa re-enact her little game with the suntan lotion. "I think I'll take a swim," she said, anxious to escape the other couple, who were lying side by side on bright red towels. Don followed her. The sea felt cool and refreshing, and she hoped it would wash away her ludicrous jealousy. She looked toward the beach and saw the two dark heads close together. An unexpected stab of pain turned like a knife in her stomach.

"Underneath it all, Vanessa may actually be a human being. What do you think?" Don joked, swimming over to where Jennifer was floating.

"I doubt it," she replied. On impulse, she put both hands on Don's shoulders and pushed, dunking him very effectively. He came up spluttering and chased her through the waves, finally managing to pay her back in kind. The physical exertion was a welcome tension-reliever. Jennifer was glad that Don was the kind of man who enjoyed horsing around.

Laughing, they swam back toward shore, then ran through the waves to get onto the beach without being knocked off their feet. Jennifer succeeded; Don didn't. They arrived back at their towels laughing. Don was covered with sand.

Stephen, Jennifer noticed with a start, seemed to be glowering at the sight of their hijinks. "I trust you kids are having a good time," he remarked sarcastically.

Before Jennifer could reply, Vanessa interrupted. "Stephen and I have had a wonderful idea," she announced, as Jennifer turned her attention to brushing the sand off Don. "Since the owner of this marvelous house isn't arriving until next week, and since he told

Stephen to make himself completely at home, let's all spend the night here! After all, it's a long, hot drive back. None of us is on duty tomorrow. So why not enjoy ourselves? We can get a few groceries in town . . ."

Jennifer's stomach felt queasy. She knew exactly what Stephen was doing. He was "taking care of the crowd," just as he had said he would. Then, late at night, after everyone else was asleep, he would come to her and . . .

She began to towel her hair vigorously to hide her panic and confusion. Why did she let him affect her that way? Yet even as she sat on her beach towel by the beautiful blue Ligurian Sea, looking to the others as if she hadn't a care in the world, she felt two bright blue eyes burning into her very soul and was torn with emotional turmoil. Every fiber in her body ached to say yes. She wanted desperately to spend the night with Stephen. But it was a completely irrational and destructive desire, and she mustn't give in to it. Just watching him with Vanessa had already proven how right she was not to trust him. Besides, she had another commitment to consider—she had promised Mary they would go to church together on Sunday.

"Well, I had a few things in mind to do tomorrow," Don was saying hesitantly, "but—"

"I'm afraid I have to get back tonight," Jennifer interrupted. "In fact, we should probably start pretty soon." She squinted up at the sun, which was already beginning to set. "I promised to take Mary Abbott to the services at the Duomo tomorrow, so I have to be there."

"Don't be silly!" Vanessa snapped. "Another Sunday will do just as well. She's a child—she'll understand—she's flexible. Don't ruin the party, Jennifer."

"But that's precisely it, don't you see, Vanessa? She *is* just a child, and she *won't* understand. I keep my promises. Especially to children. Sorry." She smiled blankly in Stephen's direction, then began gathering her belongings. "Thank you, Stephen, for letting us enjoy this house. And please don't let us rush you. We can find our way to the car, I'm sure." She started toward the stairs, leaving Don to say his good-byes.

Behind her she heard Vanessa. "Oh, don't be silly," she trilled. "I have every intention of staying. Assuming I'm still invited."

There was a deep rumble—of assent, she was sure—from Stephen. "After all, Don," Vanessa continued, "I *am* a big girl now. I don't need a chaperone. And I *certainly* don't want one!" She laughed merrily.

Jennifer was positive Stephen would have no trouble at all slaking *his* desires that evening—while she lay alone in her huge four-poster bed, wanting him but unwilling to accept his terms of surrender. She was furious to realize that tears were running down her cheeks as she reached the bottom of the stairs. She started up, two at a time, as Stephen's laugh came floating up to her.

chapter 8

As THE REVERBERATING orgàn music filled the vast space of Florence's huge cathedral the next morning, Jennifer experienced a sense of peace she hadn't felt in months. She felt a oneness with the artists who had designed, created, and embellished the structure, each one in the service of and for the glory of his own personal vision of God.

As a child, Jennifer had gone regularly to Sunday school and church in her neat middle-class neighborhood, but she had never really claimed a personal, immediate relationship with God. Here, in the company of scores of Florentines, she felt a kinship with her fellow-worshipers. They looked for and received a special kind of certainty from their religion. Jennifer hoped that a little of that sureness would rub off on her. If she could be positive that what she was doing

with her life was right...if she could really trust
another person again...then she would be happy.

She was startled by a firm but gentle hand on her
right shoulder, and her head whipped around to meet
Stephen's unique, mesmerizing gaze. She gasped in
surprise. He was crouching in the aisle, his face un-
settlingly close to hers.

"Shhhhh," he whispered, grinning. "Move over."
As he squeezed in next to her, the limited space caused
their bodies to press together. A flush of warmth
spread from Jennifer's toes to the top of her head.
Nevertheless, she noticed that Stephen was dressed
in a light blue business suit with a white shirt and a
tie. It flashed through her mind that he could scarcely
have driven from Viareggio that morning and still
have had time to change clothes. Unless he had started
very early, of course.

"How did you find us?" she hissed.

"I was outside. I saw you come in, and then I just
watched to see where you sat. Shhhh."

The choir began to sing, a glorious outpouring of
faith rising to the dome hundreds of feet above them.
Jennifer felt a soft pressure on her left hand. She
turned to Mary with a smile, expecting a wide-eyed,
awed look. Instead, she saw that tears were running
down the little girl's face.

"It's...so...beautiful," Mary whispered.

Jennifer could scarcely believe her ears. Making
a concerted effort not to overreact, she squeezed
Mary's hand in return, smiled, and said, "Yes, it is."
She stole a look at Stephen and saw that he, too, had
heard the magic words. His face had an expression
of joy and triumph that probably mirrored her own.

Suddenly she was very glad that he was there to share such a special moment with her. The tension between them seemed to have vanished. She smiled warmly, then turned her attention back to the formal, unfamiliar cadences of the service. But two thoughts filled her mind—Mary had spoken, and Stephen had come!

On the way back to the car, Jennifer didn't press Mary, and Stephen had the tact not to mention the event. He did suggest, however, that they stop at a favorite café for a *gelato*, and he insisted that they try apricot ice cream. Jennifer had never tasted it before and was delighted by the sweet-tart delicacy of the creamy confection. She savored a spoonful on her tongue as the midday sun beat on the piazza's cobblestones, releasing a scent of newly made pottery. Feeling languid in the warmth, she decided she could stay right there all day. She glanced at her companions. How easy and natural Stephen was with Mary. As she finished her ice cream with obvious relish, he spoke to her about his favorite flavors. Her eyes widened in delicious appreciation. He would make a wonderful father, Jennifer thought wistfully.

Mary looked up at the two of them. "It's very good. Thank you," she said shyly, as if experimenting with words after her long abstinence.

"I'm glad you like it," Jennifer replied. "And I'm very happy that you feel you can trust us enough to talk," she added. She had decided that *not* to comment on Mary's speech would be wrong. But she didn't over-emphasize the issue, not wanting to make Mary self-conscious.

Stephen left them at the parking lot, and Jennifer was so wrapped up in Mary that she didn't realize until he was gone that she didn't know why he had come—or when she would see him again. Back at the villa, she dropped Mary off and immediately sought out Sam and Marge. Before she could blurt out her news, however, Marge started interrogating her about the previous day.

"So tell me all about your jaunt to the beach," she demanded. "Did you remember that little restaurant?"

Jennifer smiled, accepted a cup of coffee from Sam, and wondered how to begin. "We *did* find the restaurant, and we did have fun," she said. "Actually, we met up with Stephen and Vanessa along the way, so it became something of a group effort. We stopped at a house on the coast Stephen designed a few miles north of Viareggio. Very impressive." She sipped her coffee, feeling her hard-won inner calm start to fray at the edges, and avoiding Marge's inquisitive glance. "But what I came to tell you is some good news about Mary Abbott."

Quickly and enthusiastically, she recounted her morning with Mary, neglecting to mention that Stephen had been along. She was rewarded with a hug from Sam and a resounding kiss from Marge. "That's wonderful news, Jen," Sam said softly. "I can't tell you how important a breakthrough like this can be. But don't expect too much," he warned. "She may not say anything else for some time. Let's try to keep things as they were to give her the security she'll need to keep on making progress."

As evening fell, Jennifer thought back on that conversation. Security, she mused, changing into a swimsuit. That was precisely what she lacked, why she felt so...up in the air. She had no "home" to go back to, and no financial security. No trust fund, like Vanessa. Not even a savings account.

Yet, as she strode purposefully to the pool, somehow all that didn't seem to matter. At the moment, she had something money couldn't buy—a sense of accomplishment. Slipping into the water, she realized that she was grinning. Why? she asked herself, considering her precarious position—and her unfulfilled longing for Stephen.

"Because Mary spoke to me," she said aloud, "and I'm good at what I do and I'm going to make it on my own! And also because I can deal with—" She heard a twig snap and saw a tall, familiar figure approaching from the orchards. Her heart leapt. They had shared such a wonderful moment together that morning that she felt unreservedly happy to see him.

Stephen waved and dove in. The next thing Jennifer knew, she was being dunked by a strong tug on her ankles. She broke the surface, gasping and flailing, then stroked away from him, dousing him with large quantities of water from her strong kick. He sputtered helplessly as she swam quickly to the shallow end and pulled herself up on the side.

"And what *were* you doing at the Duomo this morning?" she inquired mildly. "I thought you were still in Viareggio. I expected you and Vanessa to wait until tonight to drive back."

"Oh you did, did you?" he answered innocently. "Well, then, you were wrong, I guess. And I was at the cathedral to attend services, of course. Just like you."

Jennifer was dying to know when the two of them *had* returned—and, more important, whether they had spent the night together. But if he wasn't going to volunteer the information, she certainly wasn't going to ask.

"But let's discuss you, Mrs. Denning," he teased. "As I was crashing through the underbrush just now—so as not to startle you, you understand—I heard you say something to yourself. Do you often have conversations all alone?"

"I . . . I didn't know anyone was around," Jennifer began, then decided not to apologize. "Let's see," she continued firmly. "When we first met, you accused me of being a dreamer. In Italian, no less. Now you're accusing me of talking to myself. Since I'm clearly a mental case—and capable of resisting your charms, too—I don't know why you pay any attention to me at all!" Although she spoke the words lightly, she waited anxiously for his reply.

"Because you're a wonderful teacher," he said, suddenly serious, "and a warm, giving person. I never doubted for a moment that you'd succeed with these children, and I was very happy to share your triumph this morning." He lowered his voice. "I was hoping we'd be able to share more than that . . . again."

Jennifer's head spun at his warm response. Her stomach began to whirl as she thought of the insistent desire in his hard, passionate kiss in the bedroom of the beach house. She was sure she was blushing, but she fought to keep her tone casual. After all, he was on the other side of the pool. He couldn't touch her now and exert that almost overpowering force.

"Well, if you're referring to my spending the night at the beach house, it did look to me as if it might have gotten pretty crowded there. If you had your way, that is. And although I *am* a sophisticated divorcée, or so you keep telling me, I think three people in bed together is at least one too many."

Stephen glided calmly over to her, then abruptly pulled her into the water with strong, demanding arms.

Fighting the desire to stay in his embrace forever, Jennifer broke loose and kicked toward the diving board. Keep it light, she reminded herself, feeling a flood of warmth rushing to her toes. "Better luck next time!" she teased. Despite her triumph with Mary, she realized she was especially vulnerable right now. She had shared that victory with Stephen and felt very close to him—too close for comfort. She *had* to maintain some space or be lost again in the depths of his blue eyes, eyes that even now were becoming languid with desire.

Suddenly the image of Vanessa's smiling face, so close to Stephen's on the beach yesterday, sprang into her mind. That, and their intimate laughter following her as she ran up the stairs. She reminded herself that Stephen was used to getting what he wanted—and experienced in the means of achieving it. Just as Jeff had been. Stephen and Vanessa could have slept together and awakened early enough to reach Florence in time for the church service. Stephen's sudden appearance at the Duomo only made it clear he still wanted *her*, too. But for what? Did he have to have *both* unmarried women at the villa under his sway?

"Jennifer, why are you still fighting me?" Stephen called out angrily to her from the other side of the pool.

"Nothing has really changed since the other night, Stephen," she told him, her tone sharper than she had

intended. "I still need time and space and...
objectivity." She pulled herself up onto the diving
board and let her feet dangle in the water. Stephen
was treading water near the center of the pool.

Suddenly he swam rapidly to the side, where he
pulled himself up onto the edge of the pool. "You're
still running scared," he retorted, passing his fingers
through his thick, dark hair to keep the water out of
his eyes. "And I don't for the life of me know what
you're so frightened of. I thought, especially after
what happened in church this morning..."

His voice seemed to express genuine puzzlement,
but Jennifer looked at him stonily. Was he trying to
use the beautiful experience they had shared as a ploy
in some manipulative game he was playing? On the
beach he'd said he was proud of his powers of persuasion.

"I don't know what you want," she said quietly.
"Except sex, of course. Maybe that's *all* you want."

He opened his mouth to speak, but she held up a
hand. "I have to get back," she said quickly, jumping
up and grabbing her towel. "I have a long day ahead
of me, and I really must turn in—"

Suddenly he was beside her, his movements so
swift and sure that, before she knew what was happening, his grip was tight on her arm. He spun her
around to face him.

"You spend so much time thinking about other
people's intentions that you don't spend enough on
your own," he accused her. "Just what do *you* want,
Jennifer Denning?" He brought his face close to hers,
and she gasped. His icy blue eyes bore into hers, no

longer speaking of desire, but of determination and anger. She was too stunned to reply.

"Isn't this what you want?" he demanded, pulling her roughly against him, his mouth bearing down on hers, his tongue probing, insistent. She arched back against him, responding in spite of herself to his passionate demands. For a wild instant she remembered the rapturous abandon of their night together.

Then, just as suddenly as he'd embraced her, he thrust her away from him. She staggered backward, shocked to see mocking triumph in his eyes.

"Think about it, Jennifer," he said, his voice hard and cold. "Remember that you're never going to get what you want until you know what it is."

Filled with frustration and rage, Jennifer raised a hand to slap him. He grabbed her arm, and a dangerous glint shone in his eyes. "Now, that's something you definitely don't want to do," he said, his voice low and menacing. "It would just make me angrier than I already am."

Furious, she yanked her arm out of his grasp. Wordlessly she turned away from him and walked quickly back to the villa, her body aching from self-betrayal—and unfulfilled desire.

In the weeks that followed, Mary continued to make progress, cautiously expanding the circle of people she would talk to. At about the midpoint of the summer session, Nelson Abbott arrived from Boston for a visit. As he got out of his car, Mary flew into his arms. "Hi, Daddy!" she said in her small, sweet voice. Though he had been kept up to date on his daughter's progress, tears ran down Mr. Abbott's face when his daughter spoke. At the sight, Jennifer felt all over again her initial sense of accomplishment.

As the chauffeur unloaded the luggage and carried it to the Sandors' part of the villa, a puzzled look came to Jennifer's face.

Nelson Abbott explained. "Kurt Sandor and I are old friends, Miss Denning. In fact, we're partners in a couple of business ventures in the United States. Kurt recommended the Hastings' program for Mary, you know. Otherwise, I probably wouldn't have known about it." He smiled pleasantly. "So I'm following Kurt's suggestion and making myself at home. I'll see you at dinner."

"Yes...of course," Jennifer replied. Damn! Her every thought seemed to be instantly readable on her face. It was fortunate that Mr. Abbott didn't think her rude. And it was lucky that she was managing to avoid Stephen DiRenzo, since he was especially adept at reading her mind. Much as she hated to admit it, she missed his touch and ached to be close to him. Doubtless, he would sense that longing.

But then, she thought ruefully, even if she weren't avoiding him, she probably wouldn't have that much contact with him. For Stephen, despite his poolside lecture to her, seemed to be spending every free moment with Vanessa Ballard.

Jennifer shook her head. What she needed was a little healthy exercise to keep her mind off might-have-beens. She went inside to her room where she changed into a pair of brief white shorts and a white T-shirt, then pulled on socks and tennis shoes. As she sat at the dressing table to tie her hair back in a ponytail, she reflected that there were times when having small breasts was a blessing. She rarely wore a bra, for instance, not even when she was engaged in strenuous exercise. She took a critical look in the mirror and noticed that her nipples were faintly visible through the thin material of the plain, cotton undershirt. Oh well. Since her plan was to hit some balls against the backboard of Kurt Sandor's lovely clay court all by herself, she decided not to change. She picked up her racquet and a can of balls and left the room.

On the stairs she ran into Vanessa coming up. "Oh, Jen, do you have a game with Don or someone?" she asked.

"No, I don't. I was just going to hit a few balls, work out some kinks." She didn't have much contact with Vanessa these days, which suited her fine. She found it difficult to chat pleasantly with Vanessa since she and Stephen were probably sleeping together. She started to go past, but Vanessa put out a hand to stop her.

"Would you mind waiting for me for just a sec?" she said in a friendly voice. "I'd love to play a few games, and it won't take me long to change. Please?"

She sounded almost lonely, Jennifer thought, then instantly dismissed the idea. She smiled. "Sure, Vanessa. I'll meet you down on the court."

As Jennifer approached the fenced enclosure, entirely screened by evergreens, she heard the distinctive "thwock, thwock" of tennis balls being hit. "Oh, damn!" she muttered. For one thing, she didn't want to see anyone. For another, since the court was occupied, she and Vanessa would have to wait. She sat down on the grass, out of sight of whoever was playing.

Clasping her arms around her knees, she looked up at the tall cypress trees rustling in the gentle breeze and inhaled deeply, savoring the resiny scent of pine needles mixed with the refreshing sharpness of new-mown grass. A grin touched her lips. How easy it was to become used to this kind of life! She certainly didn't own a Vuitton tennis bag like the one she saw over by the gate to the court, and she didn't have the $100 designer tennis outfit Vanessa was sure to be wearing. But all that seemed pretty unimportant when Jennifer weighed it against what she *did* have. She stretched out on the grass. Now, if she could just stop thinking about Stephen DiRenzo, she would be content.

"Everybody up!" Vanessa's voice rang out as she rounded the turn, the green and red trimming on her white halter-neck tennis dress proclaiming it a designer original. "Who's playing?" she added just a shade too innocently.

Jennifer suddenly realized that she had been set up. But before she could object, Vanessa had bounded through the gate. Jennifer followed reluctantly. Nelson Abbott and Stephen appeared to have just finished a game.

"Hello, ladies," Nelson said expansively, wiping his brow. "Listen, this character is beating the pants off me—simply because he's ten years younger, you understand—so how about switching to doubles?" Jennifer noticed that the older man was perspiring heavily, while Stephen looked fresh and crisp, the stark white of his tennis shorts and shirt contrasting markedly with his deep tan and dark hair. His eyes seemed particularly blue, Jennifer thought, as he favored her with a quizzical glance.

But he almost immediately turned his attention to Vanessa. "I must have mentioned to you that Nelson and I were planning to play a set or two after he arrived, hmmm?" he drawled.

Vanessa ignored his tone. "Did you?" she asked absently, taking her racquet out of its press. "I really don't remember. I just saw Jennifer heading in this direction with her racquet, and I thought a little tennis might be fun. But I *don't* want to interrupt you two," she insisted, looking around, as if for a place to sit and watch.

"Don't be silly," Nelson said. "I'm delighted to be interrupted in this instance. But, to be fair, you two will have to admit which is the stronger player, because I need all the help I can get!"

"Jennifer played in college," Stephen announced in a businesslike voice, "so she's probably pretty good. I, however, haven't had the pleasure of discovering that firsthand." He paused, and his eyes moved over her appraisingly. She wished she'd worn a heavier shirt. "But I know for a fact that Vanessa has a few weak spots in her game, so she'd better play with me. Is that all right with you, Nelson?"

"Suits me fine," he replied, "but perhaps we should ask Miss Denning about her preference." How refreshing, Jennifer thought. A man who was actually going to ask her opinion about something! Before she could reply, however, Stephen got in a quick thrust.

"It's *Mrs.* Denning, Nelson. Haven't you been corrected on that point yet?"

Jennifer couldn't prevent a blush from tinging her cheeks. That creep! She felt like ramming a tennis ball right down his throat. "Please call me Jennifer," she managed in a normal voice. Pointedly, she added, "I've been divorced recently, and Mr. DiRenzo is fond of teasing me about it. However, I don't share his sense of humor on the subject."

Nelson Abbott seemed perplexed. He looked back and forth from Jennifer to Stephen. "Nor do I," he admitted, puzzled. "I wouldn't think it was a joking matter. But it isn't like Stephen to be cruel..."

Jennifer remembered that he and Stephen knew each other—Stephen had mentioned it when Mary first arrived—and she regretted her comment. "It's...it's all right," she stammered. "It's sort of a private joke, I mean. Do you want to play backhand or forehand, Mr. Abbott?"

"Call me Nelson, please," he said, obviously relieved that the tension was gone. "And I'd better play forehand because my backhand is terrible."

Jennifer sighed. She really wanted to wipe that grin off Stephen's face, but she was sure he was a very good tennis player. And if her partner couldn't hit a backhand shot...

To her delight, Jennifer managed to pull Mary's father to a 6–3 victory in the first set. As they changed sides, she felt flushed, not only with exertion, but also with triumph. Stephen *was* skilled, but his technique wasn't quite as good as hers. He was, however, faster and stronger, so he could easily overpower her if she didn't keep him off guard with sneaky shots and well-placed volleys. But by midway in the second set she realized that Nelson Abbott wasn't in shape for two sets of fast tennis. They went down to defeat, 6–4.

"I'm a generous man," Abbott gasped, sinking to the grass outside. "I won't demand a third set and humiliate our opponents. I'm perfectly willing to call it a draw. Especially if anyone knows where we might get some lemonade!" Vanessa took charge instantly, heading the foursome toward the villa where, she assured them, she would have Maria serve something thirst quenching.

Stephen came up behind Jennifer and patted her lightly on the bottom. She jumped. He held up a hand to placate her, and she was struck by the musky, masculine scent emanating from his glistening body. "That was just a congratulatory tap," he said softly, "nothing more. You play a hell of a game of tennis. And you seem to have quite a competitive streak. You must really hate to lose."

"But I'm learning all the time," she replied tightly, remembering how Stephen and Vanessa had embraced as they won the final set. She was also uncomfortably aware that perspiration made her T-shirt cling to her breasts and turned the fabric transparent. She might as well be naked, she thought in disgust. Catching the direction of Stephen's intent gaze, she draped a towel around her neck, hoping it would provide some coverage. "I'm a terrific sport, and practice makes perfect. You and Vanessa make a nice team, although," she added caustically, "her concentration seemed to be off this afternoon. I guess you have that effect on *some* women."

"Me?" he asked, sounding incredulous. "On Vanessa? Scarcely!"

Jennifer wondered for just a moment who he was trying to kid. He and Vanessa had been spending all their time together yet he denied being able to distract her? Before she had a chance to voice the sarcastic reply forming on her lips, they reached the villa, and Jennifer slipped inside and upstairs to change. When she returned, a colorful striped blouse replacing her soggy T-shirt, Vanessa was pouring tall, frosty glasses for everyone. The conversation had turned to Kurt Sandor and the villa.

"He was a brilliant eye for a deal," Nelson Abbott was saying. "Take this place, for example. As I understand it, the estate was owned by some old, respected scion of Florentine nobility who was long on pedigree but short on cash. When the prince died, his heirs couldn't afford to pay the taxes on the place. Kurt picked it up for a song. He saw the potential usefulness of the estate."

"Mr. Sandor apparently has business interests all over the world," Jennifer ventured. "How can he keep so many diverse concerns thriving?"

"By traveling a hell of a lot for one thing," Nelson replied. "I've never met anyone who spends so much time in the air as Kurt Sandor. But he seems to love it. However, he has very competent people working for him in all his offices, too. He has a reputation for acquiring talented subordinates as well as extremely sound companies. And his eye is always on the bottom line. If a manager or supervisor isn't working out, I gather that Kurt had no qualms about getting rid of that person. He's no pussycat when it comes to business."

"Sounds more like a barracuda," Stephen contributed sharply.

"I don't know him well, but he seems very kind." Jennifer was a little surprised to hear herself rising to Kurt Sandor's defense. She knew from Stephen's previous slighting comments that he disliked the man for some reason. She took an almost perverse pleasure in championing the opposing view. His glare told her she had succeeded in provoking him.

"Kurt can be enormously kind, I'm sure," Nelson said, trying to smooth ruffled feathers, "and at the same time be an extremely tough, competitive, demanding businessman. He's a hard person to make a deal with, and, once the bargain is struck, you'd better keep your end of it. So I'm delighted to have him on *my* side in the one or two deals we're in.

"Now, Vanessa," he continued, changing the subject, "I believe you were going to be kind enough to give me a brief tour? I'm anxious to see the classrooms and the common room."

"Of course!"

Jennifer was a little surprised by the eagerness with which Vanessa rose gracefully from her perch on the wall and led the way through the french doors. Since she had never shown any special interest in Mary Abbott, Jennifer assumed that there must be another reason for her enthusiasm. Was she trying to make Stephen jealous? Stealing a look at the tall architect, she noted that he seemed perfectly relaxed, enjoying his lemonade and the late-afternoon sun. He must have felt her looking at him, for he turned toward her, catching her gaze with his clear eyes. She wanted to ask him what Vanessa was up to, but he spoke before she had a chance.

"Since when have you become such a defender of our host?" he inquired once the others were out of earshot. "I didn't know you were pals with Kurt Sandor."

"We're not pals," she replied. "I hardly know the man. He was here only for a couple of days at the beginning of the summer, remember? I just found him to be very considerate and understanding, that's all. He was very sweet to me. Like a father," she added, afraid that Stephen might misunderstand.

His eyes narrowed. "A father, hmmm?" he said, almost to himself.

"Yes," she insisted, becoming irritated by his proprietary manner. "But I'm not surprised that you have some difficulty comprehending a friendship—it's not within the realm of your experience, I imagine." She changed the subject. "How do you know Nelson Abbott?" she asked. "I remember when I first met Mary that you said you knew him."

"Nelson? Oh, yes. My old firm did some work for him in Boston, and I carried blueprints back and forth on several occasions." He stood up. "I've been invited to join all of you for dinner. I trust you have no objection to eating with me under those circumstances—with lots of other people around for protection, that is?" Jennifer blushed and his voice softened, as though he wanted to call a truce. "That was quite a workout you gave me on the court, Jen. Do you suppose we could play tennis again sometime? I hesitate to ask, since you've been avoiding me so successfully, but . . ."

Tennis seemed safe enough. She was feeling self-possessed, although still cautious. "Sure, I'd like that. We're well matched."

"I've already told you that—and proved it once." He headed toward the driveway. "See you later," he called.

Jennifer's cheeks burned at his innuendo. He always managed to twist things—and to call up feelings from deep inside her that she would prefer to keep buried. She turned toward the villa and was relieved to see Sam and Marge emerging, carrying glasses of lemonade.

"Maria pressed these on us," Sam explained. "She said something about Vanessa insisting she squeeze dozens of lemons."

Jennifer laughed. "I can confirm that. She and I and Nelson Abbott and Stephen had a tennis match, and Vanessa decided to provide refreshments, courtesy of Maria, afterward." Hearing the deep roar of the Alfa-Romeo as Stephen drove down the hill, she tried to ignore the empty feeling his departure caused.

Sam and Marge settled into comfortable chairs. "I'm just delighted Nelson could make this visit," Sam said quietly. "I think it will help Mary's progress immensely to know that her father cares enough to come all the way from Boston."

Jennifer nodded. "He's an awfully nice man."

"Where is he, by the way?" Marge asked, looking around as though she expected him to materialize from under a chaise.

"Vanessa is giving him the grand tour," Jennifer replied. "She didn't even wait to say good-bye to Stephen, which seemed a little strange to me. She's completely wrapped up in her gracious-hostess routine."

"Well," Marge suggested conspiratorially, "it isn't every day that a wealthy, eligible Bostonian turns up on one's doorstep. I don't think it's the money so much—Vanessa's got plenty of that herself—but she *is* impressed by the pedigree."

"I find that hard to believe," Jennifer scoffed. "As far as I can tell, Vanessa is very much involved with Stephen DiRenzo. Now you're suggesting she's making a play for Nelson Abbott?"

"Jen, dear," Sam said gently, "I hate to gossip, and I don't mean to cast aspersions on Vanessa, who is a highly skilled professional, but Stephen DiRenzo simply isn't her type. He comes from a comfortable but not wealthy family, and though he's cultivated, sophisticated, widely traveled, and unquestionably talented, he's also a maverick—not a desirable trait in those aspiring to climb the social ladder. And he's far too independent ever to care about things like the Social Register—or the people in it. Now, while I don't pretend to know Vanessa very well, I think I can predict that Stephen is most emphatically *not* what she wants out of life."

Jennifer stared at Sam in disbelief. After all the time they'd been spending together, Vanessa and Stephen *must* be romantically involved. But perhaps the relationship was even more callous than she had suspected—based entirely on the pleasure principle with no thought of an emotional attachment or a future together. The idea repulsed her . . . but she suspected the arrangement suited Stephen perfectly.

"Would—would Nelson Abbott be interested in

her, do you think?" Jennifer asked meekly, the horrible thought suddenly striking her that Vanessa could become Mary's stepmother if she succeeded in this conquest.

"Highly doubtful." Marge sniffed, then looked at Sam, who nodded. "I don't want to break a confidence, but since you're so involved with Mary, perhaps you should know. Nelson told Sam that he's very much in love with a young woman in Boston. One of the reasons he's here is to talk with Sam about how best to break the news to Mary."

"I think he should just tell her that there's a woman in his life—and the sooner the better," Sam added. "But he seems reluctant to do that. We'll be discussing it further over the next few days."

Jennifer shared Sam's concern that Mary might very well be upset by the thought of another woman replacing her mother in Nelson Abbot's life. She felt sure, however, that he would find the right way to introduce his daughter to a potential stepmother. He was such a kind, gentle man.

No, Jennifer wasn't worried about Mary. But doubts and confusion about Stephen DiRenzo troubled her long afterward.

Alone on the terrace after dinner Jennifer was intoxicated by the sweet perfume of the moonflowers, and the breathtaking canopy of stars sparkling overhead. She felt a certain sparkle deep inside as well, which she couldn't help but attribute to the presence of Stephen DiRenzo, who was being charming and funny at the dinner table inside. She tried not to think about him and concentrated instead on the bright red sundress she was wearing. She had bought it at an outdoor bazaar for the equivalent of just a few dollars, one of her better bargains.

"You look lovely, as always," Sam said, joining her. "And also content. Since you *don't* always look content lately—much to my distress, incidentally—may I ask why you're especially happy tonight?"

"Nothing in particular, Sam," she replied, a little surprised by his observation but not eager to discuss the confusing effects Stephen DiRenzo had on her. "In fact, I was just congratulating myself on how inexpensive this dress was. In short, I was thinking about money—and you know *that* subject seldom induces contentment in me!"

"I do realize it's a sore point," he agreed. "It's too bad, really, that financial security—or the lack of it—has to play such an important role in our lives."

"I know it shouldn't, Sam," she said regretfully. "Sometimes I think I've been worrying about money all my life. One of the very nice aspects of being here with you is that so many of the annoying details are taken care of. There's no rent to pay, no groceries to buy."

"But, since we're paying such minuscule salaries, those concerns are quickly replaced by others, I imagine."

Jennifer sighed. "I worked hard to put money away every single week so that Jeff and I would be comfortable. I didn't want my children to go through the pain of having the neighbors whisper behind their backs. I still remember, after Dad died, when Mother was taking in laundry and cooking for other people." Jennifer couldn't go on. It was all so long ago, but it still hurt. Her mother had worked herself to death, she believed, getting too little rest, not eating properly, worrying too much. Sam's large, protective arm on her shoulder was a great comfort. She took a deep breath and made an effort to lighten her tone.

"It was a real blow to discover that Jeff didn't love me anymore—if he ever had. But I didn't actually hate him until I found he had appropriated our savings account and used it as a down payment on his new co-op apartment." She laughed. "An emotional betrayal followed by a practical one. After that, I wouldn't have taken a cent from him even if he'd offered. The lawyer thought I was crazy, but all I wanted was to get away. Oh, well. Starting over is something I'm good at."

Sam squeezed her shoulder. "You've got more courage than most people," he said quietly. "I'm not worried about your financial situation. But I *do* worry about the poverty of your emotional life, Jen. I'm afraid you're putting too much emphasis on safety, my dear. You've got to take some chances—even risk being hurt again. Nothing ventured, nothing gained, as they say. I hope you'll try trusting someone again soon. You'll be richer for it, I guarantee."

Jennifer smiled warmly at him. She was glad he cared enough to give her advice. But she *had* to stand on her own two feet. She *had* to be independent. "Thanks, for your concern, Sam," she said. "I'll think about it—I really will."

She and Sam moved across the terrace to join Don and Marge, who had put the students to bed. Nelson Abbott came downstairs, too, and found himself again monopolized by Vanessa. Jennifer felt a twinge of compassion for the other woman who was, after all, driven by personal demons, just as she herself was. She turned to refill her demitasse cup and nearly bumped into Stephen, who had been standing quietly behind her.

As usual, his presence unsettled her, his heathery, manly smell filling her nostrils. Sam's advice seemed emblazoned on her mind. Trust someone, he had said.

"Sneaking up on people again, Stephen?" Jennifer teased, her light tone disguising her overwhelming physical reaction to him.

"Nope," he replied seriously. "I was just watching you think. I can almost see the thoughts flying across your face. It's a fascinating pastime." He reached out and touched her forehead very gently. "What was causing all that furious mental activity?"

"Nothing that would interest you, I suspect," she replied tartly. Her tone softened. "Actually, I was thinking about money." She was astonished to hear herself admit it. "Sam and I had been talking about the sad fact that the teaching profession isn't a very lucrative one," she went on slowly, feeling her way. Would Stephen understand? "And then I realized that I don't even have enough money for a plane ticket back to New York. Not that I want to go," she added hastily. "There's nothing for me there. But I feel so . . . stranded sometimes."

Stephen looked at her intently, his eyes narrowing. "If you *had* to get somewhere, I guarantee you'd find a way," he said finally, his voice casual. "Personally, I *like* the feeling that I'm not sure where my next meal is coming from. I think that makes life a challenge.

And you know how I feel about challenges. I'd hate to be encumbered with...possessions. I'm a little surprised that someone like you would worry about such mercenary things."

His tone indicated that he found the subject of money disagreeable, that her concern with it somehow tainted her. His blasé attitude angered her. They came from such different backgrounds that it seemed he would never understand her.

"I doubt you have any real knowledge of being poor, Stephen," she snapped. "If you got in a bind, you could always sell your slick red sports car, of course, or wire Mommy and Daddy for funds. Well, some of us don't have those options, and some of us know what it feels like not to *have* that next meal. So spare me your supercilious opinions about money being beneath you!" She whirled, determined to go inside where, she realized, everyone else had settled down for after-dinner drinks.

But again Stephen caught her, just as he had at the pool, his strong hands closing around her upper arms like vises. Practically lifting her off her feet, he turned her back to face him. He looked very angry, but also sad. Despite his fierce expression and her fury, his closeness affected Jennifer like a tidal wave. Her knees gave way, and she feared she might fall if he let go.

"Is that what all this is about?" he demanded. "Your avoidance of me, your cozy little friendship with the wealthy Kurt Sandor? Don't misunderstand. I have nothing against practicality. Vanessa, for instance, knows what she wants and she's going after it. But there *is* a name for that. And I thought you were different." Abruptly, he released her arms and strode away.

As she recovered her balance, Jennifer realized she had no idea what he was talking about. Then it suddenly struck her. Even though she'd actually seen little of their gracious host, Stephen thought she was chasing Kurt Sandor for his money! She was flabbergasted!

"Stephen!" she cried in horror. He paused at the stairs. "You couldn't be more mistaken," she called out clearly, both hurt and furious that he could think that of her. Without replying, he continued down the driveway.

Jennifer was livid. How *dare* he jump to such a wild conclusion? He had absolutely no basis for it. True, she had spent some time with Kurt early in the summer, but he'd been away on business for the past several weeks.

All right then, she told herself, if that was what Stephen wanted to think, then let him. Since he already assumed the worst, why should she waste her time trying to convince him that Kurt Sandor meant nothing to her?

chapter 9

As Nelson Abbott's car disappeared down the driveway a few days later, Jennifer turned to Sam. "I'm going to miss him," she said, "and so, I know, will Mary." They walked back toward the villa as the child took Don by the hand.

"Let's go down by the pool and wave more—please?" The sight of the small girl half-pleading with and half-dragging the solidly built man caused Jennifer to burst out laughing.

"You're being manipulated by a domineering woman, Don," she called merrily as the two vanished around the corner. Her sunny mood, however, was shattered as Stephen DiRenzo turned the same corner, replendent in tennis whites and smiling cheerfully. Her heart began to pound wildly, and she wished desperately for the thousandth time that he didn't have the power to upset her so.

"Is there anyone around who feels like playing tennis?" he inquired, a gleam in his eye. He planted himself in front of Jennifer. She coolly met his eyes but couldn't tell what he was thinking. She was certain, however, that he still enjoyed teasing her. "I seem to recall that, a couple of days ago, you said you might play with me again sometime," he continued mildly. "How about now?"

"I don't think so, Stephen," she replied simply. Did he expect her to just forget what he had accused her of with Kurt Sandor? Or did he arrogantly assume that they would continue their "friendship"—if that's what it was—despite his insinuation?

"I have to go over some reports with Sam this morning," she told him, avoiding Sam's questioning look.

"I see." Stephen's eyes seemed to darken as he assessed her. Inside she felt like a schoolgirl refusing a date, but she was determined not to let him ruffle her. "Well, then, perhaps I'll see if Vanessa will favor me with *her* company," he said harshly, vanishing inside the villa.

Jennifer felt furious with him for flaunting his relationship with Vanessa. "Damn!" she muttered.

Sam ignored the expletive, put a friendly arm across Jennifer's shoulders, and walked with her to the terrace. "I haven't the vaguest idea what's going on here," he observed, "and I'm not going to ask." He paused. "There's something about Mary and her father I think you should know."

"Oh? What's that?" Jennifer asked.

"Nelson finally spoke to Mary about his plans to remarry," Sam explained. "I told him I could never offer any guarantees, but that I thought he should at least mention to Mary that he has a girlfriend. He put it off until this morning, but, as you can see, she took the news beautifully."

"Oh, I'm so glad," Jennifer exclaimed. She couldn't help asking a related question. "Since Vanessa has been wandering around like a lost soul all morning, and since she managed to miss the farewells, I gather Nelson also managed to let *her* in on his plans?"

She was pleased to see Sam's eyes sparkle. "Yes, I think he managed to drop the bad news casually in passing. He wasn't at all sure how to handle the situation."

Jennifer's jaw tightened as she remembered that Stephen had said she was like Vanessa, an adventuress out to snag a rich man. "I imagine Vanessa will land on her feet," Jennifer observed, not at all sure the wound Stephen had inflicted on her would heal as quickly. "Damn him!" she said under her breath.

"I can let one curse pass without comment," Sam noted gently, "but not two. What's the matter?"

"Sorry, Sam. It's just that Stephen compared me with Vanessa the other day, and, frankly, I was offended. I'm not a gold digger, goodness knows. If I were, I wouldn't be in such sorry financial shape! And I'm not much interested in people's pedigrees, either."

"Well," Sam drawled, "if he did accuse you of those things, then he deserves a mild damn at the very least. But let's not be too hard on Vanessa. What she's looking for is a very specific kind of security, the security of a social stamp of approval. Her father has a great deal of money, and he made it all himself. Unfortunately, in some circles that's looked down on. Vanessa's as human as the rest of us, Jen. She needs the respect of people in her circle. But I also think she has strong principles."

Jennifer didn't reply. Sam had the right to draw his own conclusions. But his next words startled her.

"Jen," he began, "I don't think Stephen and Vanessa are romantically involved, as you still seem to think. Vanessa amuses Stephen, and she can be damned good company. She's very sharp and funny. And I think she finds him an attractive and suitable escort. She has lots of contacts in this part of the world, and she's always being invited to dinners and parties given by well-known socialites."

"Well..." Jennifer was doubtful, but she had to admit that it was interesting to learn where Vanessa and Stephen had been spending all their evenings. The beginnings of their evenings, at any rate.

Her thoughts were interrupted by the deep, throaty roar of an approaching automobile. As the car came into view, she let out a sigh. It was the most beautiful machine she had ever seen. In fact, it looked like it belonged on a racetrack or, better still, a launching pad. As it pulled to a stop near the terrace, Sam let out a low whistle and walked over to the sleek silver vehicle just as Kurt Sandor slid out of the driver's seat. "Sam! Jennifer!" he called. "How nice to see you! Have I caught Nelson Abbott, or did he already leave?"

"I'm afraid he took off half an hour ago, Kurt," Sam replied, still examining the sports car. "Forgive my fascination, but I don't think I've ever been this close to a Ferrari before. This is quite a machine, Kurt. Oh, and welcome home! It's nice to have you back."

Sandor laughed. "Especially since I brought my new toy for you to admire, right? Don't worry, I'll give everyone a ride." He turned to Jennifer. "And how are you?" he asked softly. "You look wonderful, of course."

"I'm fine, thank you. We've been having a perfect summer, and the work is going extremely well, as I'm sure Sam will tell you. Will you be staying long? And how is Mrs. Sandor?"

"About the same, thank you," Kurt replied shortly. "She prefers the climate in Switzerland. For her headaches. As to staying, I'm not sure how long I can remain. But I have some business in Milan, so perhaps I'll be in and out for a couple of weeks. I wanted to see Nelson, but . . ."

"I hope you didn't have important matters to discuss with him," she said. "It's a shame you missed him. He's flying back to Boston this afternoon, I believe."

"I see. It wasn't crucial. He called the apartment, apparently, and spoke with Alicia. I was in Paris." He shrugged. "On to more pressing matters. How about that game of tennis you promised me when we last spoke? I imagine there's time before lunch."

"I'd like that," Jennifer replied enthusiastically, imagining Stephen DiRenzo's infuriating, magnetic, accusatory face on each tennis ball. "I'll just go in and change." Turning toward the villa, she discovered Stephen and Vanessa standing quietly next to the french doors. Stephen's expression was a strange mixture of anger and sadness, at once condemning and triumphant. Vanessa looked pensive.

Brushing past Jennifer to reach Kurt, Stephen stretched out his hand. "Kurt! So you've come for a visit. And arrived in style, I see." His gaze took in the luxurious automobile. "I do hope you'll enjoy your stay. And I also hope you don't mind if Vanessa and I play a quick set or two while you and . . . Jennifer are suiting up." He turned abruptly to her, and his searching eyes seemed to pierce her very soul, leaving her breathless. "Reports all done so soon?" he asked sarcastically.

"Yes," she replied defiantly, determined not to let him intimidate her. His opinion of her could scarcely be worse, after all. Or more wrong. And *he* was going off for a cozy little game with Vanessa. "I decided I deserved a break after all," she added. "Since I promised Kurt a game months ago, he's taking me up on it."

"Some people you make promises to are more fortunate than others," Stephen retorted, leaving her speechless as he walked away.

Dressing for dinner that night, Jennifer was determined to put Stephen DiRenzo and his insulting, humiliating insinuations out of her mind. Instead, she forced herself to think about Kurt Sandor. She had beaten him at tennis, but not by much. He was very quick and strong for a man of his age, extremely well-coordinated, technically skilled, and a fierce competitor. So fierce that, for a moment, Jennifer had considered dropping a couple of crucial points, worried that he would be furious if he lost. But if he felt any real rage about it, he was too good a sport to show it. Instead, he complimented her on her expertise and demanded a speedy rematch.

Jennifer looked forward to the evening meal, since Kurt would be joining them. She put on a simple green-and-white sundress that brought out the color of her eyes and slipped into low-heeled sandals.

She truly enjoyed Kurt's company, so she didn't feel any quibbles about spending time with him in order to tweak Stephen's nose. But she definitely felt no romantic interest for him, no matter what Stephen thought.

True to form, Kurt regaled them at dinner with stories of his travels. He mentioned a couple of trips to Milan in connection with an advertising agency he owned there, weekends in Germany to check quotas from some manufacturing plants there, a quick trip to Canada, where he was drilling for oil. Jennifer realized for the first time just how vast and international in scope his business empire was, and she recalled Nelson Abbott's describing him as a tough, demanding entrepreneur. She also noticed that Kurt seemed to light up when he talked about his far-flung enterprises.

"We have something in common that makes us each very lucky," she observed after dinner, as Kurt carried her cup of espresso out to the terrace for her. The others were playing bridge.

"Oh? What's that?" He sounded amused.

"We both *love* what we're doing. I could tell while you were talking about your businesses that running them gives you great joy. Reaching the children gives me the same kind of excitement and satisfaction.

We're lucky because some people work at jobs day after day that they hate. I did that for a few years myself, so I know what I'm talking about."

"Oh, really? And what work didn't give you this mysterious joy?" he asked kindly.

"I was an executive secretary at an advertising agency in New York. I did my job very well, and I certainly didn't hate it, but something was missing. I didn't get up every morning eager to get to work, the way I do now. And the way you do, I imagine."

"Have you considered the possibility that your dissatisfaction resulted from your marriage rather than the job?" Kurt suggested. "Or do you really think that this is the only kind of work that can possibly make you happy?"

Jennifer paused. She had never thought that the resentment she felt about supporting Jeff might have colored her attitude toward her job at the agency. She shrugged. "I don't know," she said honestly, "but I don't think I'll agonize over reasons and motives, now that I *am* able to do what makes me happy."

"Absolutely," Kurt agreed. "Though I feel I must defend advertising. Some people find it *very* satisfying work. Even at my agency." He laughed. "Tell me— what didn't you like about that job? Lack of responsibility? Low salary?"

Jennifer let out a hoot. "The salary was just fine, believe me." At Kurt's puzzled look, she explained, "I was making twice as much as I am now. Teaching, I find, can be a very precarious profession."

"I know how it feels to be insecure," Kurt remarked, refilling her espresso cup. "When I left my country, I had nothing. I had no idea how to get a

job, how to make money. And my English was...
rudimentary, shall we say." He shook his head and
laughed softly. "Those first few months were a time
of my life I would *not* like to repeat. And I don't
intend to." There was steel in his voice.

"What did you do?" Jennifer asked, fascinated.

"I...managed." He stared off into the darkness,
and Jennifer could almost feel his broad shoulders
droop under the weight of the memory. Then he
seemed to make a concerted effort to lighten his tone.
"Actually, I am a classic success story. I finally got
a job in the mailroom of a firm that produces machine
parts in Liverpool, and in two years I owned the company." A smile touched his lips as he shook his head.
"I make it a rule never to look back," he added,
silencing Jennifer's further questions.

Instead, she told him a little bit of her childhood
and her own experience with poverty and insecurity.
"Sometimes I feel that no one understands," she admitted. "Not even Sam and Marge. But it's important
to feel safe, don't you think?"

"I certainly do," he agreed. "I think you must strike
a balance between what you like to do—what gives
you pleasure—and what you *must* do because you are
driven. Take your situation right now, for instance.
You could make a great deal more money as a mul-
tilingual secretary. We pay our staff in Milan very
handsomely, because competent people are difficult
to find. You might think about that."

"Oh, no!" Jennifer protested cheerfully. "Thanks
for the suggestion, but I would never want to give up
teaching again." She glanced at her watch. "But if I
plan on doing it well tomorrow, I'd better get some

sleep." She held out her hand. "It's very nice that you're back in the villa," she said. "I find it so easy to talk with you."

"It's a great pleasure to be with you, my dear. Now, about the tour of my collection I promised you. Would tomorrow afternoon be convenient? We could meet out here at about three."

"I'd like that very much," Jennifer said. "I'll be here. Good night." She walked back through the french doors. In retrospect, it was too bad that she *didn't* have any romantic feelings for Kurt—he seemed to understand some of her feelings much better than Stephen ever would.

Vanessa's husky voice cut through her reverie. "I hate to be the party pooper," she said from a cozy, curled-up position in a corner armchair, where she had apparently been reading a book, "but someone should remind you that Kurt Sandor is very married, Jennifer dear. Getting involved with him can only be big trouble—and not just for you but for the Hastings School, too. After all, he is a major backer. So if you don't care about yourself, at least have a care for everyone else's job, okay?"

Jennifer was stunned. For a moment, she remained speechless, but then she pulled herself together. "For your information, Vanessa, not everyone operates the way you evidently do. Some people are able to have friendships, just plain friendships. I happen to find Mr. Sandor very kind and understanding."

Vanessa snorted, rising from the chair. "I realize you were some kind of a child bride, my dear, so perhaps you really are as naïve as you seem. Sophisticated men like Kurt Sandor aren't 'kind,' as you put it, for no reason at all."

Her words riled Jennifer. "What on earth is your problem?" she demanded, her temper beginning to boil. "Don't tell me you're jealous. Aren't Nelson Abbott and Stephen DiRenzo enough for you?"

"Speaking of Stephen," the other woman went on calmly, ignoring Jennifer's anger, "I don't think he would be altogether thrilled to know that you and Kurt Sandor are spending cozy evenings in private tête-à-têtes on dark terraces. There's a fine line between stubborn and foolish, Jennifer. Stephen DiRenzo is a terrific guy, you know, and he's absolutely mad—"

Coming from Vanessa, this advice was just too much. "I'm aware that you know Stephen extremely well," Jennifer interrupted her, "so there's no need to belabor the point. But frankly, his opinion is of no importance to me whatsoever! And neither is yours!"

"But—" Vanessa obviously had something else to say, but Jennifer didn't stay to hear it. She dashed back out onto the terrace and started down the driveway, practically running. Vanessa called something after her, but she couldn't understand the words.

The night air helped to clear Jennifer's head. By the time she reached the main road, she was laughing at herself for walking around the suburbs of Florence at eleven o'clock at night. She sat down on a low wall that bordered the road, finding the coolness of the rough stones a welcome sensation against her warm body.

The motor of an approaching car warned Jennifer

that, as safe as the environs of Florence were, a lone woman out at night was inviting trouble. She looked around for somewhere to hide until the car had passed, but no place presented itself. As the motor grew louder and louder, she began to panic.

The lights of the car rounded the last turn, catching Jennifer in their glare. Quickly she darted back up the villa driveway, stumbling in her haste. To her dismay, the car followed, gaining on her rapidly. Running now, she made it past the first bend in the driveway, panting raggedly, her heart pounding as she stepped into the bordering shrubs, praying the car would pass her. Branches whipped across her face and scratched her arms. The headlights blinded her and she stopped, frozen like a deer, as the automobile screeched to a halt.

It was the Alfo-Romeo! Stephen threw open the door and jumped out.

"I *thought* it was you I saw by the road," he said angrily, "but I couldn't be sure. What on earth are you doing out alone at this hour?"

Jennifer's relief was so great that she found herself sagging against the front fender. She took a moment to catch her breath.

"I had a little altercation with Vanessa," she finally managed to say, "and took a walk to clear my head. Then you came along, chasing me in this machine of yours, and practically scared me to death!" She was grateful to see his fierce expression fade into a look of sincere concern, his high cheekbones dramatic in the harsh headlights.

"I'm sorry," he replied, not unkindly, "but you were scampering away so fast, I thought I'd never catch you." He took her gently by the arm. "Come closer and tell me what you and Vanessa were fighting about. Although I can almost guess."

Some of Jennifer's anger returned as she recalled the conversation. "Actually, she was just continuing with the unpleasant little talks you and I have been having lately. She gave me a lecture on not consorting with married men."

"Perhaps that wasn't such bad advice," he commented.

When she started to walk away in anger again, he added gruffly, "No, don't go. Let me drive you back." He turned on the ignition and proceeded in silence.

At the villa, they sat for a moment in the moonlight.

"I'm taking Vanessa to dinner tomorrow," Stephen said. "She asked me to escort her, but I really want to get together with you, under better circumstances than these." He grinned wickedly and brushed Jennifer's cheek with the back of his hand.

She moved swiftly from the car, slamming the car door shut. "Damn!" she muttered as the Alfa-Romeo receded down the driveway. *He* could go out with Vanessa whenever the opportunity presented itself, but he expected *her* to be available and waiting for him all the other times. She wished she'd let Stephen know she was spending the following afternoon with Kurt Sandor. He deserved a taste of his own medicine.

Anger giving her energy, Jennifer climbed the stairs two at a time and let herself into her room. Turning on a bedside lamp, she found a large box tied with a bright red ribbon on her pillow. What on earth? She picked up the note that was tucked into the wrapping and opened it. "A midsummer present for a woman as refreshing as an evening breeze," it read. "For storing up security. Best, Kurt."

She tore open the package and gasped. Inside was the most wonderful piggy bank she had ever seen. Three glass pigs were nestled, each obviously hand-blown, one inside the other. The largest was about fifteen inches from snout to curly tail. The money slot was on the side of the largest pig, so coins put into the bank would eventually pile up around the interior piglets, hiding them from view.

It was an exquisite work of art, Jennifer knew— but she knew as well that she couldn't accept it. She couldn't even guess at how much it was worth, but she realized it had to be expensive.

She put the bank on the dressing table and gazed at it, sinking down in the chair. How had Kurt managed to find it in the middle of the night? It must have been in the villa. Probably Venetian glass. She noted a coin in the bottom. A dull gold, it looked very old. It, too, was probably worth a great deal of money. Oh, well. She sighed to herself. She'd tell him first thing tomorrow that she appreciated his thoughtfulness, but that she couldn't keep the gift.

chapter 10

THE NEXT DAY Jennifer found Kurt waiting for her on the terrace at the stroke of three. She felt fresh and crisp in a sleeveless white dress. He wore a colorful sport shirt, white linen slacks, and Gucci loafers with no socks. His hair was slicked back, and Jennifer suspected that he, too, had just showered. He looked older, she decided, with his hair plastered against his head. His eyes seemed smaller and closer together. But he presented a fine figure nonetheless, since his trim, broad-shouldered build was well suited to the casual sports clothes he was wearing.

Jennifer felt she had to clear up the matter of the gift right away. "Kurt," she said, taking his extended hand, "I must speak with you before we start the tour."

Instantly his expression changed to one of concern. "Is something wrong?"

"Well . . . not really," she replied. "Kurt, I found your lovely gift."

"And what do you think of it?" he asked. "A wonderful piece of workmanship, don't you agree?"

She hesitated. This was going to be harder than she'd thought, but she had to do it.

"Yes it is, but . . . Kurt—I just can't accept it. It's much too expensive."

"But my dear Jennifer, you must see by now how little money matters to me. I really want you to have it."

"No," she insisted gently. "I really can't."

To her relief, he didn't press the issue. "No, perhaps you are right." He smiled politely. "Why don't you bring it to my private rooms later, at your convenience?" His voice turned more serious. "I do hope you realize, Jennifer, that, if an emergency ever arises you can always come to me. In fact, I would be insulted if you didn't." Then, the subject closed, he placed a firm hand under her elbow.

"Shall we?"

He propelled her gently through the french doors on the private side of the villa, beginning an entertaining, casual tour of several of the bedrooms. Jennifer had worried that she would be embarrassed to invade his privacy, but she found that Kurt put her completely at ease. She didn't experience even a hint of the discomfort she'd felt when Stephen had showed her the bedrooms of the beach house near Viareggio.

And the works of art were breathtaking. A pair of della Robbia reliefs graced one of the guest rooms while another sported a frescoed wall. Jennifer was impressed not only by the depth and interest of Kurt

Sandor's collection, but also by the breadth of his knowledge.

"I am practically speechless, Kurt," Jennifer managed to say as they started back down the stairs toward the library. "Your collection is magnificent."

"Ah, but I've saved the best for last," Kurt said. "I feel that *he* provides all the drama I need in this room." Kurt directed Jennifer's attention to a portrait hanging over the fireplace.

She gasped. The face of a Renaissance nobleman, almost savage in its strength, glared down at them. The painting was so vibrant, the colors so rich and brilliant, that she couldn't take her eyes off it. She moved closer. "It's a Titian, isn't it?" she asked softly, awed by the beauty and power of the work.

"Yes," Kurt replied, coming up behind her and putting a fatherly hand on her shoulder. "Isn't he magnificent? Come, sit down for a few minutes."

She sank into one of the leather chairs, still mesmerized by the cruel gentleman in the painting. "I can understand why this is your favorite room," she said. "Though it's not a room I would choose if I wanted to be alone. It's overwhelming."

"In that case," he noted with a chuckle, "I will ring for sherry before you faint in appreciation." Alfredo soon appeared with glasses and a dusty bottle. Kurt uncorked the amontillado. "You will join me, won't you?"

Jennifer nodded, reflecting that Kurt Sandor was an extremely complicated man. She accepted a delicate-stemmed glass. "Shall we return to the terrace?" he suggested, holding out his arm. "It's a shame to waste a lovely summer evening inside, even under the gaze of so powerful a presence." He made a mock bow to the Titian as they left the room.

As they pushed open the french doors and strolled out onto the terrace, Jennifer's hand still rested lightly on his arm. He patted it in a proprietary fashion, and she was struck by how dry—almost papery—his hand felt. Just then she looked up to find Stephen and Vanessa watching them. The sudden sight of Stephen quite literally took her breath away. Her knees felt shaky, and everything but his sardonic questioning face seemed to fade into the background.

A knowing smile played on Vanessa's lips and Jennifer refused to pull her hand away from Kurt's. After all, here was Stephen with Vanessa.

She smiled with false brightness. "Hello, Stephen, Vanessa," she called. "Kurt has just given me a tour of some of his collection. It was a real treat."

"Speaking of treats," Vanessa said, "guess where Stephen and I are dining tonight." Jennifer grimaced. Leave it to Vanessa to draw any conversation to herself. "Sabatini's," she informed them triumphantly.

"Ah! Sabatini's!" Kurt exclaimed. "The best Florence has to offer. Or it used to be. I'm sure you'll enjoy it."

Stephen laughed. "I definitely plan to enjoy it since Paolo, Vanessa's friend, is picking up the tab! The food *is* good, but even *you* have to admit, Kurt, that the prices are outrageous."

"I don't know, really," he said thoughtfully. "I haven't been there this summer, so I'm not familiar with what inflation has done to the menu." He thought for a moment, then turned to Jennifer with enthusiasm. "But we can certainly remedy that! My dear, if you're not 'on duty' tonight, would you do me the honor of joining me for dinner? I think you would enjoy it, and I know *I* would."

Jennifer looked up, startled, to see a scowl flash across Stephen's face. Kurt's invitation *had* caught her by surprise, but Stephen had no right to look put out.

"What a wonderful idea," she said gaily to Kurt. "I'm not on tonight, and I'd love to go out to dinner with you."

"Fine. I'll call Gianni and tell him to make room for us, and I will bring the car around a little after eight. Until then?"

Sabatini's was even more elegant than any of the fancy New York restaurants Jennifer had frequented during her ad-agency days. Masses of flowers, banked for maximum effect around a stunning display of cold antipasti, filled the foyer with their perfume. Another table was filled to the edges with luscious-looking fruit tarts, bowls of berries, and other confections. Here and there, gleaming service carts stood guard, waiting for the headwaiter to whip up a *fettucine Alfredo* or a *zabaglione* tableside.

The captain approached them, elegant in his dinner jacket. "Signor Sandor, *che piacere,*" he enthused. "What a pleasure to see you. And the signora—*che bella donna*. What a beautiful woman." Jennifer felt her cheeks color at the compliment. Then she caught sight of Stephen and his group seated at a prominent table. Throwing her shoulders back, she took Kurt's arm as they swept past the others to a corner booth with a commanding view of the entire room.

She was seated facing Stephen, just a couple of tables away, while Vanessa, fortunately from Jennifer's point of view, had her back to the entire room. Jennifer found it hard to concentrate on the dinner, or the conversation. Much to her chagrin, she found herself yearning for Stephen. He looked so handsome in the dark formal suit and crisp white shirt, and he moved with such controlled strength, as if he were chafing under the restrictions of civilized behavior. It was almost impossible to keep her eyes off him, but every time she looked his way, he caught her glance.

"I hope you're enjoying the evening, my dear," Kurt said gently as the waiter brought espresso for both of them.

"Oh, yes!" she replied, making a renewed effort to focus her attention on Kurt. "When *you* plan something, it proceeds so smoothly—or at least that's the way it seems to me. There are no hitches, no problems. Everything is always perfect. Do you know what I mean?"

"Of course," he said kindly, choosing a cigar from the humidor the waiter offered. "Having things function efficiently is very important to me. In business, it is crucial. On an evening as pleasant as this one, it is important. Not that anything tragic could go wrong, but it really is so easy to make sure everything goes right. So I do."

She glanced over toward the other table and noticed that the very nice-looking middle-aged man, who was presumably Paolo Rinaldo, was just settling the check. As Stephen rose and approached their table, Jennifer feared her heart might stop. She wanted to say, "I don't like this game anymore, Stephen—please take me home!" But she kept still.

"Is the food still up to your standards, Kurt?" he asked, ignoring Jennifer.

Kurt took a puff on his cigar before smiling pleasantly. "It certainly is. And the company is even more delightful than the cuisine. I hope you three enjoyed your dinner as well?"

"Yes, indeed," Stephen replied, a little stiffly. "Well, good night, then." For a moment Jennifer thought he wanted to say something else—wanted to say something to *her*—but instead he turned and walked quickly out of the restaurant.

She cleared her throat, fighting her disappointment, and turned to Kurt. "Tell me about Vanessa's new prospect—Paolo Rinaldo, is it? Have you ever met him before?"

"Many times. Rinaldo's a good shipbuilder," Kurt commented dryly, "and he also has an eye for the ladies. Which is why his wife divorced him, I believe." He signaled for the check. "But now, I had better get you home. I'm sure you have a busy day tomorrow, and I know I do."

That night Jennifer woke up suddenly, feeling disoriented. She looked at the clock. Two-thirty. She remembered the lovely dinner, the drive back, the way Kurt had kissed her hand gently as he left her at the door. On impulse, she had given him a light kiss on the cheek. It had been a pleasant end to a pleasant evening. So why was she awake now? And then she smelled the heathery scent. Her heart leaped.

She sat up and was reaching for the bedside lamp

when a firm hand covered her mouth. "Don't scream—it's Stephen," he whispered urgently. She relaxed, but could still feel the adrenalin pumping into her bloodstream. Fear was mixed with the special kind of excitement Stephen's mere presence elicited in her.

He took his hand away cautiously. "You nearly gave me heart failure," she hissed. "What on earth are you doing creeping around my room in the middle of the night?"

"We have to talk, Jen." His voice was low and urgent.

"What's wrong with talking in the daylight?" she replied testily. Warning bells were going off in her head. She mustn't let him stay here. Already she felt herself responding to his closeness, and she was uncomfortably aware of the very sheer sliplike nightgown she was wearing. She pulled the sheet up around her.

"For all I know, Kurt has some new house-and-garden tour planned for tomorrow," Stephen complained.

"He's driving to Milan tomorrow. You and I can talk then." She had to get him out of the room! Her head was whirling, and a languid warmth seemed to be filling her veins.

"No, I want to talk now," he said, his voice husky. In the faint moonlight, she saw that he had removed the jacket and tie he'd worn at dinner, and that his shirt was unbuttoned halfway down, revealing his smooth, tanned, muscular chest. She longed to touch him, to trace the contours of his body. His strong scent filled her nostrils.

For what seemed an eternity, he held her gaze,

mesmerizing her with his intense blue eyes. Slowly his eyes fell to her long throat and pale shoulders, gleaming like marble in the silvery light. His gaze traveled lower to her creamy breasts, clearly visible through the transparent gown. Jennifer sat as still as a statue, transfixed by his power over her.

At last his eyes returned to her face. "You're right, Jennifer," he whispered, his voice low and gentle, "it's not a good time to talk. That can wait until tomorrow. Tonight—right now—I want to make love to you. But I won't force you. I won't seduce you. I won't touch you until you touch me...This time, Jennifer, you must come to me."

As if in slow motion, she shook her head. "No, Stephen, please don't ask me to do that." Her eyes pleaded with him, but his expression remained unchanged. "Please, Stephen...I want to make love to you, but I can't...I can't..."

"Tell me why," he demanded urgently. "You know what to do. Jennifer, I need you so badly."

And suddenly she could resist him no longer. That one word—*need*, instead of *want*—shattered the last barrier between them. He didn't love her, but he needed her, and her own love for him made it necessary that she fulfill that need as best she could.

It was she who reached out to him as all the yearning of that evening rose like a flood within her. She touched his face with trembling fingers and then his firm warm lips, and then her own lips replaced her fingers, and suddenly she was in his arms as a little cry of joy escaped her. She touched him everywhere, reveling in his smooth skin over taut muscles, and, as he caressed and stroked her in return, she grew oblivious to time, lifted on a tide of pure emotion. She kissed his shoulder and his neck as he slid down and applied his soft but powerful lips to her small round breasts. "Oh, yes!" she breathed.

She wasn't aware of any pause in their lovemaking, but suddenly she felt the naked length of him pressed against her. She was gasping for breath, and he put his hand, now infinitely gentle, over her mouth again. "Shhhh, my sweet," he murmured. "I want to make this wonderful for you, but I don't want to wake the rest of the household in the process."

She looked at him helplessly, drowning in his beautiful blue gaze. He kissed her mouth, her ear, her neck, then moved down to the hollow beneath her collarbone, then her navel. She swallowed a moan, thinking that she had never felt such exquisite sensations. She twisted around and began running her fingernails, ever so lightly, across his back and down and around his firm, tight buttocks. When her efforts were rewarded by a gasp from Stephen, she increased the pressure a little, reveling in the giving of pleasure.

But her own pleasure was reaching unendurable heights as they became entwined together on the large bed. Her every nerve ending seemed to be on fire, crying for release. "Oh, please," she moaned, "please, Stephen . . ." And suddenly they were together, moving in unison to create an ecstasy so perfect that Jennifer thought she might lose consciousness. The waves washed over her, one after another, and she bit her hand to keep from crying out.

They were both completely drenched, she realized sometime later as she felt her senses slowly begin to return to normal. But nothing would ever be the same, she thought, looking at Stephen's face on the pillow beside her. His eyes opened and he smiled. "I love you," she said, tracing his cheekbone with her finger.

His arm tightened around her. "And now you're mine," he said with satisfaction. "Utterly, completely mine. Or are you too liberated to be possessed?" he teased.

She tensed. Possession and domination were always uppermost in his mind. But before she could speak, he moved to the edge of the bed and began pulling on his socks. "I think I'd better slip away now," he said lightly. His sudden departure from her side disoriented her. Surely he couldn't be leaving so soon.

"But I don't plan on making a habit of such quick departures," he was saying. "I think we should talk to Sam and Marge about your moving into my cottage for the rest of the summer. I can't imagine they would object, unless there's some problem connected with the kids. But if we're reasonably discreet, I don't think there'll be any difficulties."

Jennifer stared at him incredulously. "We're going to have to talk about all this, Stephen," she began, but he had already moved to the dressing table and had switched on a light. She blinked in the harsh glare.

"What's this, Jen?" he asked, indicating Kurt's gift. "I know you have a thing about saving money, but a piggy bank?"

"Kurt gave it to me," she said absently, still upset by his suggestion that they live together. He acted so nonchalant, as if he moved in with women every day.

"I should have known." Stephen's angry tone recaptured her startled attention. He set the fragile object back on the dressing table with a force that made Jennifer wince. His voice was deceptively mild as he crossed over to the bed. "I'll just bet you and Kurt had a long heart-to-heart at some point about money and about how scared you are by a lack of financial security, and then he gave you this." His voice turned harsh, and his eyes were icy. "You want to have your cake and eat it, too, is that it? But if dear old Kurt knew you were sleeping with me, he might not be so generous."

His words cut her to the quick. How could he insinuate something so harsh and cruel? How could he after what they had just shared? He had turned into a mocking stranger before her very eyes. "Get out of here, Stephen!" she said with cold fury. "Get out and don't ever come back."

"Don't worry," he said. "I won't." In an instant he was gone.

Jennifer stared numbly at the closed door. She had sent him away. In a moment she would remember why. Right now she couldn't seem to think. She felt so empty inside.

Overwhelmed with sudden weariness, she stretched out beneath the sheet and stared blankly at the ceiling as tears fell silently from her eyes.

chapter 11

THE FINAL MONTH of the summer term seemed end-
less. Jennifer rarely saw Stephen, except in passing,
or when he stopped to pick Vanessa up for some social
engagement. On those occasions he was polite, even
friendly, but distant. Jennifer could scarcely believe
he was the man who had twice made love to her so
rapturously, who had made her feel sensations she
had never thought possible.

Kurt Sandor was away on business most of the
time, dropping by only occasionally and never for
more than a quick drink before dinner. Jennifer
couldn't help but feel somewhat embarrassed around
him, knowing what Stephen thought of them. She had
returned the piggy bank to Kurt the day after her
breakup with Stephen and now was careful not to
spend time alone with him.

But she wished she felt able to confide her deep hurt to someone. She couldn't talk about it even with Sam and Marge, who, like everyone else, were giving their utmost to the children as the term drew to an end. Jennifer was grateful for the opportunity to immerse herself in her teaching.

Sitting on the terrace one early evening in late August, she reflected that at least one good thing had happened during the summer. The staff's commitment to the Hastings School and its students was really paying off. Mary Abbott was practically a chatterbox now. It was almost as though she were making up for lost time. The others had made significant progress as well.

Jennifer glanced up as Sam and Marge joined her on the terrace, carrying glasses and a bottle of wine. The day had been hot and humid, and Jennifer felt as though the air itself was an added weight on her shoulders. "A small drink before dinner, Jen dear?" Marge asked as Sam plied the corkscrew.

Jennifer nodded. "Thanks. I was just thinking about the students. Each one has done so well . . . Do you know yet which of them will be back in the fall? Has Nelson Abbott decided anything about Mary?"

"Not yet. I think he's torn because he's delighted with the progress we've made—I should say, *you've* made—but he misses her terribly. Once he gets his personal life squared away and sets the date for his wedding, I think he'll see things more clearly. But quite a few of the others will be back."

"The fact is," Sam interjected softly, "we're completely filled for the fall term. We'll have a fascinating group of students, Jen, and our staff will be expanded to include three more people from the United States, plus a British teacher whom Marge and I were hoping could come. You'll love her. It's going to be a wonderful year, Jen."

She smiled a little sadly, wishing she could share Sam's enthusiasm wholeheartedly. "That's marvelous news, and I *am* looking forward to the fall term."

"Then why do you look so glum?" Marge inquired gently. "For the last several weeks, you've seemed a little depressed."

"I'll . . . I'll be sorry to see people go, that's all," she managed. "I'm not very good at endings, in case you hadn't noticed."

"I know you're concerned about Mary," Sam said, "but I can't think who else's departure could be making you gloomy. Don *is* going back to the States, but just for the holiday break, and I scarcely thought Vanessa's imminent departure would fill you with despair . . ." Sam had just the hint of a twinkle in his eyes as he refilled her wineglass.

Jennifer laughed in spite of herself. "Vanessa and I really haven't gotten along too well, have we?" she said wryly. "I must say that I think her decision to return to doing pure research is a wise one. She isn't the type to get her hands dirty rolling around the floor with real kids. But I was surprised to hear that she had wangled a grant to do some work at the University at Basel. That's quite close to Genoa, isn't it? Isn't that where Paolo Rinaldo is from?"

"Absolutely," Marge declared. "With connections going back to popes and kings and who-knows-what. He's a count or something, I believe, which someone told me is better than a prince in Italy, because there are a lot more princes than there are counts. Or was it the other way around?" She paused for a moment. "And what about you?" she asked, "I thought for a while that you and Stephen might..."

"There's nothing there," Jennifer replied, a little too hastily. "Except some pretty unpleasant friction, I'm afraid. We just seem to rub each other the wrong way."

"That's too bad," Sam remarked thoughtfully. "He's an extremely fine young man. And he has certainly done his job for us with skill and efficiency. Did you know that the construction has been completed? They moved the last of the heavy equipment out yesterday. All we need now is a little landscaping and it will be perfectly charming. Have you seen it lately?"

"No, I haven't. Not for...weeks. Has...Stephen left, then?" Jennifer couldn't bear the thought that he might have left without saying good-bye...without giving the two of them even a hint of a chance to work things out. The fear that he was gone forever lay like a leaden lump in the pit of her stomach.

"I don't think he's gone," Marge answered cheerfully. "Though, when I saw him the other day, he said he was packing up. I expect him at our little farewell party on Friday. Sam and I are looking forward to us being together for one last time before we head for a vacation in Sicily."

Out of consideration for Marge, Jennifer nodded, but she really didn't look forward to Friday's party at all. It would mark the end of another term's work in her life, a life that seemed dedicated to work alone.

Oh, not that work didn't have its rewards...she would remember the first time Mary had spoken for the rest of her life. But Stephen's absence had shown her with painful clarity that she needed more than just work...

The party would be hard for another reason, of course. Stephen would be there, his mocking eyes and sensitive lips tormenting her with thoughts of what might have been. But there was no use wishing for things that just couldn't be. She'd make it through the party on Friday on sheer will, if necessary, the same way she'd made it through the past year.

Friday dawned, a stunningly brilliant day. Bright rays showed around the edges of her drapes, and the sound of bustle in the hallway brought Jennifer to full consciousness. She glanced at her clock—ten-thirty! She hadn't overslept like that in years. She hurriedly threw on some clothes, and rushed out into the corridor, only to find herself face-to-face with Vanessa, a juxtaposition that was possible only because the small brunette was wearing extremely high heels.

As always, in an encounter with Vanessa, Jennifer made a positive effort to call on all the good manners she had been taught since childhood. She managed a polite smile. "I understand you're going to be doing some research in Switzerland. Congratulations."

"Thank you," Vanessa answered. "This summer has taught me a number of things, and one of them is that my gifts, such as they are, do not include teaching. I like kids, really I do..." She sounded wistful. "But I'm much more successful with laboratory animals. So the research position is a stroke of luck. Especially since it means I don't have to be too far from Paolo."

Her smile was almost shy, and Jennifer was startled by the honest, disarming nature of her confession. Had Vanessa changed so radically? Or had she misjudged her? Vanessa was wearing a most becoming— and uncharacteristically conservative—yellow linen dress, cut like a shirt and belted casually at the waist. On most women the bright color would have made them look sallow, but it only served to enhance Vanessa's becoming tan.

"And what a pretty dress!" she couldn't help saying. "I haven't seen it before. Is it new?"

"Thanks again," Vanessa replied sincerely. "As a matter of fact, it is. Paolo and I are driving to Milan tonight, then flying to Athens in the morning. We're going to spend a few weeks cruising the Greek islands."

"Lucky you!" Jennifer felt her guard relaxing. Apparently Vanessa's interest really *was* shifting away from Stephen. "I've only seen pictures, but Greece looks like one of the most beautiful places in the world."

Vanessa reached out and touched Jennifer's arm lightly in a gesture of friendship. "You know, we're the only two here," she said. "Sam, Marge, and Don took the last of the kids off to the airport just after seven this morning and won't be back 'til late afternoon—just about when the servants come on to get things in final shape for the party." Her expression grew serious. "Look, Jennifer, why don't we get some breakfast together for you, and the two of us can talk. I think we have a lot to say."

Jennifer felt herself tightening up again, but she couldn't very well refuse. What in the world did Vanessa have to talk with her about?

A few minutes later they were settled on the terrace, a steaming cup of *caffè-latte* and a buttered roll in front of Jennifer. Vanessa didn't waste any words.

"Jennifer," she began, "we just have to talk about Stephen."

"There's really nothing to say about Stephen as far as I'm concerned," she protested softly. "There's nothing between us. We haven't even had a real conversation in weeks."

"I know," Vanessa said. "That's what I want to talk to you about. He's miserable, and so, I suspect, are you. First of all, let me say that he and I were never . . . involved. Though perhaps he liked to tweak your nose by making you think so."

Jennifer flushed as Vanessa continued. "When I found out he was with *you* when I had to call him about the Monte Carlo problem, and that he never explained what all that was about—well, I was just furious. But he wouldn't let me tell you. Jennifer," she leaned toward her, "Paolo has a home there. Something went wrong with the renovations that Stephen designed, and when Paolo couldn't reach Stephen at his home, he called the school. As a last-ditch effort, I called that restaurant, knowing it was one of his favorites."

"Vanessa," Jennifer said, surprised at how controlled her voice sounded, "I'm glad to know the truth—I must confess I *was* wondering about all that—but I really don't think it's going to make that much of a difference. Stephen has just totally avoided me recently—"

"But don't you see," Vanessa interrupted eagerly, "that's why you *have* to talk! He told me he saw a very expensive present that Kurt Sandor had given you, and that he just exploded."

Jennifer narrowed her eyes, but there was no hint in Vanessa's expression that Stephen had described the specific circumstances of his discovery. "He certainly did," she said mildly. "He jumped to some pretty nasty conclusions, too, and didn't give me a chance to explain." She decided to tell Vanessa the truth. "As a matter of fact, as soon as I saw the gift, I decided to return it. But I guess Stephen isn't the only stubborn person around here. For a while I really did want him to think that Kurt was some kind of rival," she confessed, then smiled bitterly. "I guess it worked only too well."

Vanessa glanced quickly at her watch, then rose. "Listen Jennifer, I've got to dash. Paolo will be out front in a minute. But please, you've got to speak with Stephen. Things will work out—I know they will." She leaned over to kiss Jennifer on the cheek, then darted into the house.

Jennifer remained alone on the terrace for a while, staring into her coffee cup. Did she trust what Vanessa had just told her? She had certainly sounded sincere. And she seemed like such a different person today. Jennifer began to doubt her previous judgment of Vanessa. Perhaps Paolo's love—for she was beginning to think they really did mean something to each

other—had softened her. Jennifer gave a quiet, bitter
laugh. She, on the other hand, only became more
sharp-tongued in the face of cupid's darts. But then,
she reflected, look at the men she'd loved—Jeff and
Stephen. Both knew exactly what they wanted out of
life, and were willing to use her to get it.

Was Vanessa right about Stephen, or was she only
trying to play matchmaker now that she herself was
settled? Was Stephen a kind of consolation prize?

Immediately Jennifer upbraided herself. There she
went again, suspecting everybody's motives. She'd
better get a little peace and quiet before the party, or
she'd never make it through it. With new determination, she dashed upstairs to her room and changed
into a daring lavender bikini she hadn't even worn
yet. She headed for the pool without even bothering
to take a cover-up. After all, she was sure that no one
was around today, not even the staff.

At poolside she decided to rest a minute in a chaise
longue. She closed her eyes, enjoying the gentle
breeze. Peace at last...

"Scusi, signora."

At the sound of the familiar voice, her heart did
a flip-flop. Her eyes flew open. Stephen DiRenzo
stood before her, looking elegant and cool in a beige
linen suit and a navy-blue silk shirt. She willed herself
to sit up slowly, to keep her face an indifferent mask.

He cleared his throat. "I think I have a lot of apol-
ogizing to do," he said. Indicating a lawn chair next
to the chaise, he asked, "Mind if I sit down?"

"Of course not," she replied, although she felt
wary.

"First of all, I think you'll be pleased to hear that

I had a long talk with Kurt Sandor. He told me about you returning the bank."

Her eyes flashed angrily. "Oh, so I suppose that means I'm forgiven in your eyes? Well, that's nice to hear, but I don't want your approval, okay?"

To her surprise—and indignation—he laughed in response to her outburst. She started to get up.

"Whoa," he said, taking her gently by the arm. Merriment lit up his eyes. "How many of our conversations have ended with me trying to nab you on the run?"

"Quite a few," she admitted hotly, "and for good reason. I refuse to suffer an entire conversation with you and your recriminations, your one-sided view of everything I do."

A serious look came over his face. "Please," he said, "you're right." He pulled her gently back down to her seat. "Can I tell you a story?"

"About what?" Despite his change in expression, she didn't particularly feel in the mood to listen to him any longer. Just being in his presence hurt enough.

"You've told me a lot about your past, and I appreciate that. Not many people can be honest about an experience like yours with Jeff. It's hard to learn that someone you love doesn't love you back. Or, even worse, is using you." He looked down as he said the last words and sighed deeply. "You see, Jennifer, I always thought I had too much pride to let anyone know about my past, about the woman I once hoped to marry."

She looked at him, surprised by his statement and his tone. This wasn't the mocking, self-assured Stephen DiRenzo talking. "Marry?" she repeated softly. "When was this?"

He laughed bitterly, making her cringe inside. She wanted to reach out to him, to run a soothing hand along his arm, but she wasn't sure how he would react to it at that moment.

"When? Two years ago," he said. "I spent the summer and fall working in New York for a prestigious Park Avenue firm, and I met a woman, Marion, who had just come to work for the same firm. She was an architect and also had an MBA, and she was a beautiful blonde." Stephen paused. "Everyone was crazy about her. The partners in the firm adored her, all the underlings loved her, even my mother thought Marion was great. And so, after about two months, she moved into my apartment."

Jennifer tensed instinctively, then forced herself to relax and let Stephen explain. He went on.

"We were very happy. Or so I thought. We shared the same interests and, although I sensed she was more in tune with the corporate life than I was, I thought we were the perfect match. After another month, I asked her to marry me. She said 'Sure,' but it would have to wait awhile because her calendar was full. We both laughed."

"And..." Jennifer prompted. Seeing how hard it was for him to go on, she laid a hand on his arm and was struck by the hardness of the muscle under the whisper-smooth silk shirt.

"Marion was doing very well with the firm, getting all the plum assignments and traveling a good deal. I didn't feel that we were competing in any way. She would make little comments—like my office was an island of serenity, really off the beaten track. I thought she liked it that way, that she could retreat from the rat race when she was with me. As it turned out, I guess she just thought I had no ambition."

He stopped to collect his thoughts, then plunged ahead. "Anyway, it got to be Christmas, and I wanted to announce our engagement. So I bought her a ring.

"Meanwhile, the office gossip mill was working overtime. The senior partner was divorcing his wife of twenty-five years. It was *the* topic of conversation at the Christmas party. Afterward, Marion and I went to our favorite little neighborhood restaurant, and I gave her the ring. She said—I'll never forget the words—'How sweet, Steve, but I'm afraid I can't accept it.' In a perfectly pleasant, cheerful voice. I asked why not, and she said, 'Because Jack and I are flying to Haiti tomorrow,'—Jack was that senior partner I mentioned—'And after he gets his divorce, we're getting married. And I'm starting a branch office for the firm in Chicago. I do hope you understand,' she said, 'because you and I aren't right for each other at all.' And she calmly finished her dinner while I sat there stunned. As she left, she mentioned that she had already packed her things and moved out of the apartment. 'Thanks for the use of the bed!' was her parting comment."

As Stephen finished, the air was thick with silence. He glanced at her, and she saw that his eyes were filled with the memory of the pain of his loss. She knew the same pain was in her eyes whenever she thought about her marriage with Jeff.

No wonder Stephen resented driven, wealthy older

men and considered them rivals, Jennifer thought, amazed by his story. And no wonder he had reacted so negatively to her insistence on being independent, or putting her career first. "You must have been terribly hurt," she said softly.

He got up and walked away. "Most of all, I was mad as hell," he answered. "I've never been so furious with anyone. But by the time I recovered my wits, she was gone. I had put my trust in a faithless, conniving, ladder-climbing woman, and she used me. Betrayed me. Sold me out. I very nearly quit the firm then and there, but I figured that was the coward's way out."

He returned to Jennifer's side and searched her face intently. "But that's in the past. I'm determined to put it behind me, and I will. I've let it get between us for too long already. And I've missed you terribly."

Jennifer's heart lifted at his confession. "I'm so sorry for all the awful things I thought about you," she said. "For all the doubts I had. Jeff had hurt me too much to trust you. Stephen, I—I . . ."

He put up a hand to stop her. "No." He sighed. "No, it's still my turn to talk, Jen." His blue eyes looked down into hers, and the pain that had been in them just moments before had changed to an exquisite tenderness. Jennifer gasped. The care expressed in those eyes made her feel like a rare treasure. "Jennifer, I thought all along that pride kept me from telling you this. Well, that wasn't exactly right. It was foolishness. But I've learned that in someone as bull-headed as I am the only thing that outweighs foolishness is love." He took her into his arms, and she rested her head against his hard chest. An unbelievable calm filled her, a sense of indescribable joy at the touch of his light, feathery kisses on her hair.

"Jen, I realize now that Kurt Sandor meant nothing to you, but I want you to know that Vanessa never meant anything special to me. I took her places because she needed an escort, and...well, you and I weren't on very good terms a lot of the time, were we? But from the very beginning you were the only one I wanted. The only one I cared about...You do believe me, don't you?"

Looking up at him, she *did* believe him. For the first time she trusted him utterly. He would never use her as Jeff had. And because he, too, had known the pain of rejection, he would never knowingly hurt her. She was free to love him as she yearned to do...

Could this really be happening to her? she wondered. Could she really have found this kind of happiness at last? As if in answer to her unspoken question, Stephen pulled back, keeping his hands on her shoulders.

"Jennifer," he said, his eyes seeming to reach down into the depths of her soul, "there's no denying it—we're both old-fashioned people, and we believe in old-fashioned institutions. How would you like to turn tonight's farewell party into an engagement party?"

She gasped in delight. "You mean you want to marry me?" He nodded, chuckling. "Oh, Stephen," she cried, "I never dared dream it could ever happen, but yes, yes, I will marry you."

"Well, then," he said, "we'd better get into Florence to get a ring. And how about some place real exotic for a honeymoon?" A devilish gleam came into his eyes. "Hmmm...how about Rome?"

She poked him in mock exasperation. "You, *Signor* DiRenzo, are asking for trouble. You're lucky I don't push you, snazzy European clothes and all, into the pool."

"The pool..." Both of them looked at the cool, beckoning water, and seemed to get the same idea at once.

"Last one in is a rotten egg!" Giving a deep, rich laugh she hadn't allowed herself in ages, Jennifer ran to the pool and dove in cleanly. She floated on her back, kicking gently across the pool until she reached the far edge, then hooked her arms up over the rim to watch her soon-to-be fiancé remove the last of his clothes before making his own expert dive.

He surfaced beside her and playfully undid her bikini top, then reached underwater to undo the two ties that held in place the last barrier between them.

His eyes were full of mischief. "Come to think of it," he said, "I find I'm not really in that much of a mood for a swim." He nuzzled her neck gently.

"Mmmm," she responded, running her hands up and down his sleek back. "Come to think of it, neither am I."

"Nobody's around," he said. "We could just slip across the field to a cozy little cottage I know about." His eyes were daring her.

Meeting his gaze boldly, Jennifer pulled herself out of the pool, leaving her bathing suit behind, and wrapped herself in a towel. Stephen calmly followed, his bronzed body glistening in the sun as he twisted another towel around his waist. He grabbed her hand. "Let's run!" he shouted.

Laughing and stumbling in their haste, they ran hand in hand across the sun-warmed field that lay between the villa and Stephen's cottage. As they entered the cool, dimly lit interior, breathing hard, their gazes met and held.

"I love you, Stephen," Jennifer whispered into the soft shadows.

"And I love you, Jennifer," he answered solemnly.

As he touched her cheek, Jennifer was amazed to see that his fingers were trembling. And then she forgot this new evidence of her effect on him because he was taking her into his arms and setting her whole body on fire.

His lips began to devour hers as though he were a starving man, his tongue exploring all the secret recesses of her mouth. She buried her hands in his hair, pressing him against her, careless of the towel that fell to the floor, revealing her naked body glistening with perspiration. His own towel followed as he carried her to the bed. As he stretched out next to her, she moved closer, impatient to feel his warm, hard chest against her bare breasts.

His hands were kneading her back, her breasts, her buttocks, then slipping down between her legs. "Oh, Stephen," she moaned, "I want you so . . . I've missed you terribly . . ." Her hands travelled up and down his back, luxuriating in the contours of his firm, muscular body. Suddenly he rolled over onto his back, and she found herself on top of him. She stretched out on his chest, tracing the planes of his face with gentle fingers.

Their breath was coming in gasps, and the moment of calm was short-lived. Soon they were rolling over and over on the bed, their bodies intimately entwined. Panting, Jennifer tried to breathe deeply, but she couldn't. His lips were everywhere, turning the flame of her desire into an uncontrolled blaze. She was making incoherent animal sounds, completely oblivious to anything but the searing sensations of the moment. All the agonies and doubts of the past few weeks were erased by the overpowering rush of passion as Stephen made wild and unforgettable love to her, raising her to higher and higher peaks of joy.

When Jennifer awoke much later, it was dark outside, but the cottage was illuminated by candles and an oil lamp. Stephen was kneeling by the tiny refrigerator, taking out a bottle of wine and a bowl of fruit. As he caught her eye, he smiled broadly, then returned to the bed and settled down beside her. "Feeling rested?" he murmured, kissing her eyebrow.

"Not entirely," she confessed, stretching like a cat. Her body ached in the most pleasurable way, and the scents of their passion still filled her nose. "We missed the going-away party." She sighed as he handed her a glass of wine. "Do you mind?"

"No. Now, where were we," he asked, arching an eyebrow, "when we were so pleasurably overcome by desire?" He kissed her again, a sweet, lingering kiss on the lips.

"I love you," she murmured against his mouth, "and I've wanted you so much..."

"And you'll have me," he whispered. "Now and forever." He stretched out next to her. "If we made a few, quick phone calls, my parents could fly over tomorrow," he said between kisses, "and Sam and Marge could come back from Sicily." He kissed her collarbone. "And we could all meet in Sardinia and get married next Saturday."

"Oh, yes," Jennifer sighed, squirming with pleasure as he began caressing her body again, gently and expertly. "Yes, yes, yes." Her breath was coming in tiny gasps.

"Oh, and I quit my job at the firm," he told her, kissing the side of her breast, "because Nelson Abbott has hired me to design a house for him and his new bride—and Mary, of course. And after that there's another commission on Capri, and then there's the work Alicia Sandor wants me to do in Cortina d'Ampezzo. So, if we're willing to live simply, at least until we start having babies, I think we can do just fine financially. Especially if we settle near Florence so you can stay on at the school. Okay?"

"Oh, Stephen, it's much more than okay. It's perfect."

"Good," he concluded firmly. "Then the only thing left to do is get some sleep so we can begin making arrangements tomorrow morning." She nodded happily and snuggled into the warm curve of his body. "Jennifer, we won't get much sleep if you don't stop that," he warned her as he leaned over and blew out the lamp. She laughed and reached for him in the dark, fully satisfied when his arms tightened around her.

WHAT READERS SAY ABOUT
SECOND CHANCE AT LOVE BOOKS

"Your books are the greatest!"
—*M. N., Carteret, New Jersey**

"I have been reading romance novels for quite some time, but the SECOND CHANCE AT LOVE books are the most enjoyable."
—*P. R., Vicksburg, Mississippi**

"I enjoy SECOND CHANCE [AT LOVE] more than any books that I have read and I do read a lot."
—*J. R., Gretna, Louisiana**

"For years I've had my subscription in to Harlequin. Currently there is a series called Circle of Love, but you have them all beat."
—*C. B., Chicago, Illinois**

"I really think your books are exceptional...I read Harlequin and Silhouette and although I still like them, I'll buy your books over theirs. SECOND CHANCE [AT LOVE] is more interesting and holds your attention and imagination with a better story line..."
—*J. W., Flagstaff, Arizona**

"I've read many romances, but yours take the 'cake'!"
—*D. H., Bloomsburg, Pennsylvania**

"Have waited ten years for *good* romance books. Now I have them."
—*M. P., Jacksonville, Florida**

*Names and addresses available upon request